Making Light of Tragedy

JESSICA GRANT

The Porcupine's Quill

Library and Archives Canada Cataloguing in Publication

Grant, Jessica, 1972–
Making light of tragedy / Jessica Grant.

Short Stories
ISBN 0-88984-253-1

I. Title.

PS8613.R367M35 2004   C813'.6   C2004-903561-4

Published by The Porcupine's Quill,
68 Main Street, Erin, Ontario N0B 1T0.
www.sentex.net/~pql

Readied for the press by John Metcalf; copy edited by Doris Cowan.

Represented in Canada by the Literary Press Group.
Trade orders are available from University of Toronto Press.

We acknowledge the support of the Ontario Arts Council
and the Canada Council for the Arts for our publishing program.
The financial support of the Government of Canada
through the Book Publishing Industry Development Program
is also gratefully acknowledged. Thanks, also
to the Government of Ontario through the Ontario
Media Development Corporation's Ontario Book Initiative.

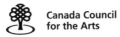

Canada Council   Conseil des Arts
for the Arts   du Canada

Canadä

ONTARIO ARTS COUNCIL
CONSEIL DES ARTS DE L'ONTARIO

Table of Contents

My Husband's Jump

My husband was an Olympic ski jumper. (*Is* an Olympic ski jumper?) But in the last Olympics, he never landed.

It began like any other jump. His speed was exactly what it should be. His height was impressive, as always. Up, up he went, into a perfect sky that held its breath for him. He soared. Past the ninety- and hundred-metre marks, past every mark, past the marks that weren't really marks at all, just marks for decoration, impossible reference points, marks nobody ever expected to hit. Up. Over the crowd, slicing the sky. Every cheer in every language stopped; every flag in every colour dropped.

It was a wondrous sight.

Then he was gone, and they came after me. Desperate to make sense of it. And what could I tell them? He'd always warned me ski jumping was his life. I'd assumed he meant metaphorically. I didn't know he meant to spend (*sus*pend) his life mid-jump.

How did I feel? Honestly, and I swear this is true, at first I felt only wonder. It was pure, even as I watched him disappear. I wasn't worried about him, not then. I didn't begrudge him, not then. I didn't feel jealous, suspicious, forsaken.

I was pure as that sky.

But through a crack in the blue, in slithered Iago and Cassius and every troublemaker, doubt-planter, and doomsayer there ever was. In slithered the faithless.

Family, friends, teammates, the bloody IOC – they had 'thoughts' they wanted to share with me.

The first, from the IOC, was drugs. What did I think about drugs? Of course he must have been taking something, they said. Something their tests had overlooked? They were charming, disarming.

It was not a proud moment for me, shaking my head in public, saying no, no, no in my heart, and secretly checking every pocket, shoe, ski boot, cabinet, canister, and drawer in the house. I found nothing. Neither did the IOC. They tested and retested his blood, his urine, his hair. (They still had these *pieces* of him? Could I have them, I wondered, when they were done?)

The drug theory fizzled, for lack of evidence. Besides, the experts said (and why had they not spoken earlier?) such a drug did not, *could not*, exist. Yet. Though no doubt somebody somewhere was working on it.

A Swiss ski jumper, exhausted and slippery-looking, a rival of my husband's, took me to dinner.

He told me the story of a French man whose hang glider had caught a bizarre air current. An insidious Alpine wind, he said, one wind in a billion (what were the chances?) had scooped up his wings and lifted him to a cold, airless altitude that could not support life.

Ah. So my husband's skis had caught a similarly rare and determined air current? He had been carried off, against his will, into the stratosphere?

The Swiss ski jumper nodded enthusiastically.

You believe, then, that my husband is dead?

He nodded again, but with less gusto. He was not heartless – just nervous and desperate to persuade me of something he didn't quite believe himself. I watched him fumble helplessly with his fork.

Have you slept recently? I asked. You seem jumpy – excuse the pun.

He frowned. You don't believe it was the wind?

I shook my head. I'd been doing that a lot lately.

His fist hit the table. Then how? He looked around, as if he expected my husband to step out from behind the coatrack. *Ta da!*

I invited him to check under the table.

Was it jealousy? Had my husband achieved what every ski jumper ultimately longs for, but dares not articulate? A dream that lies dormant, the sleeping back of a ski hill, beneath every jump. A silent, monstrous wish.

Yes, it was jealousy – and I pitied the Swiss ski jumper. I pitied them all. For any jump to follow my husband's, any jump *with a landing*, was now pointless. A hundred metres, a hundred and ten, twenty, thirty metres. Who cared? I had heard the IOC was planning to scrap ski jumping from the next Olympics. How could they hold a new event when the last one had never officially ended?

They needed closure, they said. Until they had it, they couldn't move on.

Neither, apparently, could my Swiss friend. He continued to take me to dinner, to lecture me about winds and aerodynamics. He produced weather maps. He insisted, he impressed upon me ... couldn't I see the veracity, the validity of ... look here ... put your finger here on this line and follow it to its logical end. Don't you see how it might have happened?

I shook my head – no. But I did. After the fifth dinner, how could I help but see, even if I couldn't believe?

I caught sleeplessness like an air current. It coiled and uncoiled beneath my blankets, a tiny tornado of worry, fraying the edges of sleep. I would wake, gasping – the *enormity* of what had happened: My husband had never landed. Where was he, *now*, at this instant? Was he dead? Pinned to the side of some unskiable mountain? Had he been carried out to sea and dropped like Icarus, with no witnesses, no one to congratulate him, no one to grieve?

I had an undersea image of him: A slow-motion landing through a fish-suspended world – his skis still in perfect V formation.

Meanwhile the media were attributing my husband's incredible jump to an extramarital affair. They failed to elaborate, or offer proof, or to draw any logical connection between the affair and the feat itself. But this, I understand, is what the media do: They attribute the inexplicable to extramarital affairs. So I tried not to take it personally.

I did, however, tell one reporter that while adultery may break the law of *marriage*, it has never been known to break the law of *gravity*. I was quite pleased with my quip, but they never published it.

My husband's family adopted a more distressing theory. While they didn't believe he was having an affair, they believed he was trying to escape *me*. To jump ship, so to speak. Evidently the marriage was bad. Look at the lengths he'd gone to. Literally, the *lengths*.

In my heart of hearts I knew it wasn't true. I had only to remember the way he proposed, spontaneously, on a chair lift in New Mexico. Or the way he littered our bed with Hershey's Kisses every Valentine's Day. Or the way he taught me to snowplow with my beginner's skis, making an upside-down V in the snow, the reverse of his in the air.

But their suspicions hurt nonetheless and, I confess, sometimes they were my suspicions too. Sometimes my life was a country-and-western song: Had he really loved me? How could he just fly away? Not a word, no goodbye. Couldn't he have shared his sky ... with me?

But these were surface doubts. They came, they went. Like I said, where it counted, in my heart of hearts, I never faltered.

The world was not interested in *my* theory, however. When I mentioned God, eyes glazed or were quickly averted, the subject politely changed. I tried to explain that my husband's jump had made a believer out of me. Out of *me*. That in itself was a miracle.

So where were the religious zealots, now that I'd joined their ranks? I'd spent my life feeling outnumbered by them – how dare they all defect? Now they screamed *Stunt*, or *Affair*, or *Air current*, or *Fraud*. Only I screamed *God*. Mine was the lone voice, howling *God* at the moon, night after night, half expecting to see my husband's silhouette pass before it like Santa Claus.

God was mine. He belonged to me now. I felt the weight of responsibility. Lost a husband, gained a deity. What did it mean? It was like inheriting a pet, unexpectedly. A very large Saint Bernard. What would I feed him? Where would he sleep? Could he cure me of loneliness, bring me a hot beverage when I was sick?

I went to see Sister Perpetua, my old high school principal. She coughed frequently – and her coughs were bigger than she was. Vast, hungry coughs.

Her room was spare: a bed, a table, a chair. Through a gabled window I could see the overpass linking the convent to the school. Tall black triangles drifted to and fro behind the glass.

You've found your faith, Sister Perpetua said.

I couldn't help it.

And then she said what I most dreaded to hear: that she had lost hers.

I left the window and went to her. The bed groaned beneath my weight. Beside me, Sister Perpetua scarcely dented the blanket.

She had lost her faith the night she saw my husband jump. She and the other sisters had been gathered around the television in the common room. When he failed to land, she said, they felt something yanked from them, something sucked from the room, from the world entire – something irrevocably lost.

God?

She shrugged. What we had *thought* was God.

His failure to land, she continued, but I didn't hear the rest. His failure to land. *His failure to land.*

Why not miracle of flight? Why not leap of faith?

I told her I was sure of God's existence now, as sure as if he were tied up in my backyard. I could smell him on my hands. That's how close he was. How real, how tangible, how furry.

She lifted her hands to her face, inhaled deeply, and coughed. For a good three minutes she coughed, and I crouched beneath the swirling air in the room, afraid.

It was a warm night in July. A plaintive wind sang under my sleep. I woke, went to the window, lifted the screen. In the yard below, the dog was softly whining. It was not the wind after all. When he saw me, he was quiet. He had such great sad eyes – they broke the heart, they really did.

I sank to my knees beside the window.

I was content, I told him, when everyone else believed and I did not. Why is that?

He shook his great floppy head. Spittle flew like stars around him.

And now all I'm left with is a dog – forgive me, but you are a very silent partner.

I knelt there for a long time, watching him, watching the sky. I thought about the word *jump*. My husband's word.

I considered it first as a noun, the lesser of its forms. As a noun, it was already over. A completed thing. *A* jump. A half-circle you could trace with your finger, follow on the screen, measure against lines on the ground. Here is where you took off, here is where you landed.

But my husband's *jump* was a verb, not a noun. Forever unfinished. What must it be like, I wondered, to hang your life on a single word? To *jump*. A verb ridden into the sunset. One verb to end all others.

To *jump*. Not to doubt, to pity, to worry, to prove or disprove. Not to remember, to howl, to ask, to answer. Not to love. Not even to *be*.

And not to *land*. Never, ever to land.

Bellicrostic

The people at the party were characters from the man's novel. Or the characters in the man's novel were people at the party.

When she finally met him, the man, the author, she said, I read your novel. Then I moved in.

He said, You're not the first person to say that.

This had been at another gathering, mostly writers, and there were smiles all around the room.

This happens, they agreed.

Yes, and then you're not a writer any more.

BELLICROSTIC
Spring 1999. Volume 36.

Submission guidelines:
We welcome up to 5,000 words of typed, double-spaced unpublished work. We regret that we no longer accept stories about substance abuse. Please include a self-addressed, stamped envelope. Allow one to three months for a response.

BELLICROSTIC
Winter 2000. Volume 39.

Submission guidelines:
Send no more than 5,000 words of typed, double-spaced unpublished work. We regret that we no longer accept stories about substance abuse or domestic violence. Nor do we accept stories that celebrate cultural identity or mourn the loss thereof. Please include a self-addressed, stamped envelope. Allow one to three months for a response.

BELLICROSTIC

Winter 2001. Volume 43.

Submission guidelines:

We do not accept stories about substance abuse or domestic violence. We do not accept stories that celebrate cultural identity or mourn the loss thereof. We do not accept stories about survival. Please do not send stories with epigraphs. 2,000-word limit.

BELLICROSTIC

Summer 2001. Volume 45.

For submission guidelines, please refer to our web site. We regret that we no longer accept stories with metaphors. If your submission contains a metaphor, we will not return it.

Do you think you need some time off?

Marcel was in her doorway. He pushed his forehead into the doorjamb. It's not that I'm not *with you* on this, Deborah. We all are – God knows. But this could be the end. I mean, you can't send out an issue with blank pages – and (he pointed two fingers at her) don't tell me that's not what you want to do – ultimately.

She raised her hands in the air. Guilty.

I know it. But Deborah, people *subscribe*. People pay money to read this stuff.

I've become so – she sighed and looked at the word tacked up on her office wall – so *bellicrostic*.

We all have, darling. But we can't continue this way. You know what will happen? I'll tell you. They'll start sending metafiction. Cute, self-referential pieces. Flash fiction if you keep cutting the word limit.

Please God no.

I'm just saying.

All literature is passive-aggressive, she decided.

Not surprisingly, she had a brief love affair with an interactive computer game. She first played 'The Sims' at Marcel's. It works like this: You create and control a suburban family. You decide what they look like. You name them. You set them up in a house, buy furniture and appliances. You make all their decisions: when to sleep, when to shower, when to shit. You let them drink coffee, or you don't. Status bars tell you how they're doing. The Dad's energy level is low. The Mom needs social activity. The Kid is hungry – is always hungry.

Marcel loaned her the CD and she installed it at home.

She made mistakes at first. Forgot to put in a fire alarm. The stove caught fire. She let the Dad stay home from work and he lost his job.

But she learned. Soon they were making money, making friends, improving themselves. The Mom was in politics and practised her speeches in front of the mirror, accumulating charisma points. The Dad improved his mechanical skills by reading books about mechanical skills. He could fix the cappuccino machine and unclog the toilet.

There were neighbours too – the Goth family – who dropped by, or who could be asked over, for companionship. The Goths came with the game.

She discovered an option that allowed her to play the Goths, rule *their* roost for a while. Her first bird's-eye view into their home stunned her. The Goths were rich. Their house was worth ten times what she could afford for her own family. They had a piano, a pool, a garden. Worse, they had taste. A colour scheme in each room, artwork on the walls, coordinated appliances in the kitchen. They put her to shame.

Her first reaction was to ransack. She removed bits of their home. She could do that. She confused them, made them miserable. Then she put the stuff back.

She was bored. Bored with her family, bored with the Goths. They were all just existing. She tried to get a homosexual relationship going between Mortimer Goth and her family's Dad. The game wouldn't allow it.

She could let them die, she realized. Let them lose their jobs, live in filth, forbid them to eat. But that would be a slow process. They were a healthy, increasingly self-sufficient bunch.

She finally told Mortimer Goth to get in the pool. He was happy to oblige. His Fun status bar surged. She paused the game and removed the ladder to the pool. That's how easy it is: Murder. You just delete the ladder. Then resume the game. Mortimer kept swimming his laps. His energy dropped. He was hungry. He had to go to the bathroom. He wasn't having fun anymore. Sorry, friend. All the status bars were in the red. It got dark. He started waving frantically – at *her*. At Deborah.

She watched him die. When he gave up the ghost (which is literally how the game depicts death; a dirge plays and the character becomes transparent and floats away), she put back the ladder and called the mother out to the pool.

Deborah killed the entire family.

She was sick with shame when it was over. She would uninstall. Soon. But first she moved her own family into the Goth's house. Let them have their day in the sun. Then she put them in the pool too.

I've done it all, she told Marcel. I'm finished.

There's an expansion pack you should try, he said. 'The Sims Unleashed'. Bigger neighbourhood, better clothes, more friends. And pets. You can have pets now.

There's no religion in that game, she said. And you can't have a homosexual relationship.

They're working on that.

Yeah? And in the meantime? How do they expect to keep us interested? How do they expect to keep us ethical?

The novel had been about a community of authors, and by virtue of being what it was, and being it brilliantly, it robbed those authors of authorship. Bestowed charactership. Ingenious. The last good novel she'd read.

There were times when she was called upon to write something other than submission guidelines. A book review, say, or a speech.

What if I'm illiterate?

A long night would follow, with her thinking up ways to conceal her illiteracy. Eye problems were her best bet. She would feign blindness while she learned to read. *Hooked on Phonics* tapes in the car. What car? You're blind. Right. Which raised another issue: How convincing could she really be, as a blind person? What about the first insect she instinctively swatted away? What about looking into someone's eyes, in a crisis, unable to help it?

Or she could be honest. There was always that. She'd call a meeting. She'd say, I'm illiterate. I don't want anyone to panic. I'm taking a course. I'm still the same old Deborah – witty, charming, bellicrostic. I just need a little time. To get up to speed.

How long does it take an adult to learn to read? To become super-literate. Literary-journal literate. How long?

But she wasn't illiterate, of course. The next morning, she'd pick up a submission, some piece about a dying way of life, and the words would cozy up to her like a cat, over-familiar. She would remember: This is what it is to read.

Dean of Humanity

I am not very nice to the cab driver. He doesn't know where the gallery is, so we have to pull over, flip on the interior light, and pore over a map.

I ordered the cab *five hours* in advance. I know – who does that? But in the winter, during peak hours, all the representatives (i.e., the dispatcher) tend to be 'busy helping other customers'. So I called at 2:00. Which meant I spent five hours waiting. Not in any obvious way. I wasn't down on the sidewalk until 6:50, ten minutes before the scheduled arrival time. But the waiting really began the moment I hung up the phone. You know how that is.

So at 6:50 I was on the sidewalk in front of my building, waiting. 7:05 came and went. No cab. I hurried back upstairs. Sorry, no record of my 'order', said the dispatcher. Irony in the voice. When did you say you called? Around two. For a seven o'clock cab? Yes – so how long? Twenty minutes. Fuck. Okay. Back downstairs, waiting. And it's minus fifteen degrees.

I begin to feel anxious as the distance between me and my apartment unfolds and complexifies. The cab driver's map is a book of maps. The city is not, as you might wish, a coherent, connected layer. No, the city is many hundreds of layers, and we must ascend and descend through all of them until we find the one we're looking for. I calculate I am at least thirty pages from home now. Thirty-one, thirty-two. The fare is $20 and climbing.

The cab driver feels it unnecessary to heat the interior of his cab. We sit in a cloud of our own breath. I push my hands deep into my mittens.

I hate him.

The reading is sponsored by the university and couldn't be further from the university. Art Space turns out to be a gallery-cum-warehouse in the middle of nowhere. The fare is so much that I won't have enough to get home. I will have to use a credit card for the cab fare home. Assuming another cab can find this place.

I try to calculate the tip, but I can't do math in someone else's presence. This is why I could never play Yahtzee. I ask the driver to step outside. He won't. Finally I tip him an exorbitant amount. I'm sorry for hating you, I say. Yeah, he says. No problem. So he knew? And now I love him a little.

I dash inside, and I've missed nothing because these things never start on time. The Dean of Humanities has not yet introduced the man who will introduce the reader.

There is so much space in Art Space that I am a very small planet with no trajectory. I drift over to the table selling the writer's book. The table is something to orbit. I make three revolutions and carry on to the far end of the room, where chairs are filling up.

I take a seat at the end of a row and remove my mittens, hat, scarf, and coat. I make a careful pyramid on my lap. To my right is a work of art: a giant green bicycle. Do I like it? Yes. Very much. I take a deep breath.

Why can't the Writer in Residence stay *in residence*? Why must he be Writer out of Residence, Writer in Art Space?

It isn't his fault. I locate him in a corner. He will have to ascend a staircase to read. I watch him now, assessing that staircase. At the very top is a podium, quite near the ceiling. What kind of arrangement is this? He is quaking. Does anyone else see it? No. The audience is chatty. Drinking wine. Wine? I turn in my chair. A bar. I missed the bar. But now it's too late. Besides, I couldn't manage a glass of wine *and* my pyramid of outerwear. Must keep things simple.

So. Introductions begin, the subject of which is not the writer or his work, but the university that brought him here. Aren't we lucky? Isn't he lucky?

Not if he has vertigo.

The writer ascends the stairs.

I'm wondering why I came. Because I love literature? No. You can't love anything so vast as that. I love my desk and my halogen lamp and sometimes I love what I see when I look down through a page. When the page is like water.

But listening to someone read, what I hear usually is saliva. Especially when a microphone is used. So no, I just came to be brave. To leave my desk so that I might return and say: *See.* I was out for a while.

The Writer in Residence clears his throat. He begins a story of a world emptied out, or perhaps a world not yet found. His unempty voice builds an empty world. How? I don't hear saliva. I forget about stealing the green bicycle and riding it home. The Writer in Residence makes silence out of sound. How?

When he is finished, he is intercepted on the stairs by the Dean of Humanities. Will you take a few questions from the audience? The writer declines, politely. But he will be happy to answer questions one on one. Say, over a drink.

I am already up and into my coat. Hat, mittens, scarf. To find a phone and call a cab.

So it happens that the Writer in Residence and I collide at the bar. We know each other, sort of. We met when he first arrived in the city. I do not ask him: Cold enough out there for ya? Because he is sweating. There are little drops on his forehead.

He says, I looked for your story in the *Malahat Review.* The library doesn't have that issue.

My story? You looked for it?

Sure.

Aw shucks.

And truly I am touched. Harried and sweaty as he is, having just read from an Olympic height, the Writer out of Residence has thought to ask *me* about my single published story.

Drink? he asks.

No, but thanks. Actually, I'm looking for a phone. I make eye contact with the bartender. She points at a door that says Staff Only. I begin to back towards it.

So, I say. Great reading.

Slide that story under my door, he says.

Hey – I point two fingers – I'll do that.

The Staff Only room is the real story. Ratty carpet. A crescent of pita bread by the phone. I take a quick bite. Yeah. Could you send a cab to Art Space? What do you mean, you don't know where that is? I find that very hard to believe. (Nervous laughter, mine.) It's on 26th Avenue South East. How long? Twenty minutes. Fuck. Okay.

I wait outside. It's minus twenty. I can just tell. I walk up and down an itty-bitty strip of sidewalk, maybe ten feet long. Sidewalk as decoration. When was the last time Art Space saw a pedestrian?

A guy I know, sort of, a grad student, steps outside in a T-shirt for a cigarette. Hey, he says. Leaving? Yeah. Smoking? He half-laughs, exhales. Someone's looking for you.

Who?

The Dean of Humanities. I think. The guy with the bow tie.

Shit. What for? I'll miss my cab.

I'll keep watch.

Okay.

I hurry back inside. The place feels very crowded now. When people drink, they multiply. I can't find the Dean. I circle the room three times, then exit. T-shirt smoker is gone. No sign of my cab either.

I continue pacing the sidewalk. I'm pretty sure the cab came and left while I was inside. I'm pretty damn convinced. Should I call again? What if it arrives while I'm making that call? I'll take that risk.

Been there and gone, says the dispatcher.

What?

Been there and gone.

Fuck. Send another, will you?

Twenty minutes.

I hang up.

There's always the bicycle.

But it's artwork.

Back outside. It must be minus thirty.

I wonder what the Dean of Humanities wants with me. We know each other, sort of. We serve on a committee together.

The door opens. A scarf conceals his bow tie, but I'd know him anywhere.

Ah, there you are, he says, happily slapping his gloved hands. Mon dieu it's cold. He is French, the Dean, but speaks flawless English.

Minus thirty, I tell him.

I thought you might need a lift.

I've called a cab. But thank you. That's very kind.

Pffff. I will drive you, he says. Come.

I couldn't. An imposition. It's out of your way.

Where do you live?

Near the university.

Art Space. The university. My house. It's a matter of making a triangle. Come.

I hesitate. Yes, but a big triangle or a small one?

The Dean of Humanities drives a compact car with a stick shift. We zip out of the parking lot and, within two minutes, on that dark and empty road back to the city, we pass my cab.

The Dean points.

Oh well.

We discuss the reading, sort of. The gallery (A wonderful space, non? Yes, the green bicycle – I'm a fan). Respectable turn-out. Yes. Book sales. Yes.

After a moment, he says, And all is going well for you, Nicole?

Yes. Fine.

A big adjustment, moving to a new city, attending a new university.

I think of my desk with its lamp. Not really, I say. I like where I live.

The car warms up. As the distance between me and my apartment collapses, I relax. Ten pages away now, by the cab driver's map. Or so I imagine. We are unreading the space to safety.

The Dean tells me about his niece who is visiting from France. She's here for six months to improve her English. She's studying to be a war correspondent.

I picture the war correspondents I know from the *National*. Adrienne Arsenault in Jerusalem. Paul Workman in Iraq. Often they wear flak jackets. I can't concentrate on what someone is saying if they're wearing a flak jacket. Instead I watch the roofs behind them.

Your niece must be very brave, I say.

She has wanted to be a war correspondent since she was a little girl.

This conjures another image – a French child speaking into a hairbrush. Behind her, mother and son do battle over his refusal to eat cheese.

Unusual, I say.

We are on the outskirts of campus.

You must direct me from here, says the Dean.

The familiarity of my surroundings makes me overeager, almost festive. I give the Dean more information than he needs. There's a Lutheran Church just down the block. You'll see that first. Then a senior citizens' home. Then a tower. In a moment, you'll see the tower. That's where I live.

When he pulls up outside my building, I feel like ruffling his hair. Thank you so much, I say.

You are most welcome.

I undo my seat belt.

Oh – one more thing, Nicole.

I look at him. My building, lit up like a Christmas tree, tips in his glasses.

Perhaps you'd like to come to dinner next Saturday? he says. You could meet Mélanie. I've invited Tom also.

Panic. Who? The names feel like math.

My niece.

Oh. And I realize he means Tom from tonight, Writer-in-Residence Tom. Next Saturday?

I just thought, he says. You don't know anyone here. Neither do they. He makes his hands into scales, as if weighing us against each other. An idea, he says. That is all. My wife and I are magnificent cooks. You will see.

I nod.

So you will come?

I punch my mittens together like boxing gloves.

One should not be all the time alone, Nicole. Forgive me for saying so.

We've turned a page. Like the cab driver's map. This one has a larger scale. The Dean and his house loom very large.

No, I say. Meaning I agree. One should not be all the time alone.

You will come then?

Yes, of course. Thank you.

Why did I agree to that?

A shadow of worry now. I lie in bed and imagine how it will go. The niece will wear a flak jacket. And she will be very brave. She will want a new best friend for the six months she is here. I will be interviewed. The Writer in Residence, out of residence, will sweat. The niece will take very long strides around the house. She will produce atlases. The Dean of Humanities will wear a chef's cap, and his wife will lift it from his head when we sit down, *à table*. His wife will have earrings like road maps.

No, I am seeing maps because I am almost asleep. The maps come unbidden. Along with that feeling of universal waiting. The whole planet poised on the edge of *next*.

Even in sleep I am waiting. All sleep progresses toward waking, and this longing for it guides my sleep.

The niece, Mélanie, *is* wearing a vest that looks remarkably like a flak jacket. Sometimes, when she speaks, she holds her fork at an angle, not unlike a microphone. But reporters don't hold microphones anymore, do they? No. I've invented the fork-as-microphone connection. There is none. Mélanie is merely animated.

I am reading your book, Tom, she says from behind her solid blue vest. I think you must have written it for me?

Tom laughs, makes a vague figure-eight pattern with his chin, as if to say yes and no, yes and no, I have no idea what you mean.

It is about waiting to depart, she explains to the rest of us. It is about departures. Mine. She places a hand with the fork over her bullet-proof heart. And I will have many. I am always waiting to go, go, go. She laughs.

My wineglass is dirty. I can feel the grit of past meals under my hand. On the rim, a faint print of lipstick not mine. I look across the table at Gloriana, wife of the Dean of Humanities. I match her lips to the print on the glass. The traces of food are baked on, the mark of an ineffective dishwasher. I pick at them like scabs. I press my own lips over the print.

Gloriana wears something asymmetrical that is partly a dress, partly pants. She jingles when she moves, which she does a lot. She and Mélanie share this. Animation. They accessorize with whatever is handy – here at the table, cutlery. Her earrings are not road maps but yawning silver rings with concentric circles turning inside. Solar systems, better than ours.

Earlier, when she announced that she was a fan of science fiction, addressing this to Tom as a sort of compliment, her earrings became solar systems. Prior to that, they were just elaborate mobiles. But then she talked about outer space and I began to see her earrings differently.

Tom, meanwhile, looked bewildered.

It was Mélanie who picked us up, in the Dean's car. I was not expecting this. I saw the car. I expected the Dean. I jogged down the walk from my building, hopscotching over the ice patches. There was Tom in the passenger seat. I recognized him. But no Dean.

Salut, said the war correspondent, angling a hand into the back seat. I shook it. My uncle is busy cooking our dinner. Canard à l'orange.

She pulled a quick U-turn and we left my building behind. She wore a hat with dangling ear flaps and gloves with no fingers. Her window was slightly open. The ear flaps blew in the wind.

We were just talking, Tom said, about the metric system.

Yes, said Mélanie. You have not fully embraced it here. She took her hands off the wheel to make a wide embracing gesture.

We've been half-assed about the metric system, Tom said, as if he felt truly guilty about it.

Half-assed? said Mélanie.

Tom's coat made some noise in the front seat. He was moving around inside it. Half-hearted? he said.

Reluctant, I said.

Ah. Half-assed. Yes, you have. For instance, do you weigh in kilos?

This went on until we'd exhausted all units of measurement.

I was dismayed by the length of the drive for two reasons. One – the obvious one – because I was further from my apartment than I'd anticipated. And two, because the Dean had misled me about the size of the 'triangle' he was required to make in order to drive me home the other night. I had been an inconvenience after all.

So Nicole, Mélanie was saying, how do you know my uncle? You are one of his students?

No. We're on a committee together. Does he teach too? I didn't realize.

Oh. Perhaps not. I always forget – a magic movement with her ungloved fingers – that now he is the Dean of Humanity.

Tom and I looked at her. She'd said the Dean of Humanités, I supposed. The S silent. But Tom was nodding to himself. I could tell he liked it. So did I.

The Dean had assumed a new status.

The house is not as grand as it should be. It is not a house befitting the Dean of Humanity. Oh, there is much exposed wood. But there is something of the hotel lobby about the living room. The furniture hugs the floor, overstuffed. The lamps are hot and brassy.

Before dinner, we had drinks in the living room, and the chair the Dean sat in clashed with his bow tie.

And now, in the dining room, the wineglasses are too delicate. They should be goblets. Yes, large dirty goblets we should be drinking from.

And the walls should be red velvet.

At the Dean's table, we form allegiances.

Tom and me, because we are out of residence.

Mélanie and me, because we are the same age and gender.

Gloriana and Mélanie, because they share the same political views.

Gloriana and Mélanie, because they use cutlery to emphasize said political views.

Tom and me, because we are political lightweights (though, in my own defence, my ignorance is partly due to my inability to concentrate on war correspondents' broadcasts, when flak jackets are worn).

Tom and Mélanie – because here there is a subtle flirtation happening, sparked by the suggestion that he wrote his book for her – which Tom appears to now be seriously considering.

And over it all, the Dean of Humanity presides. It is impossible to become his ally, his favourite, though clearly this is what we all want. Our conversation is a performance, a jockeying for his esteem. Oh to make him laugh. (Mélanie: Let's just say I put your little car through its paces. D of H, rolling his eyes: Oh mon dieu.) To please him. (Me: This duck is divine. D of H: I am so glad.) To touch him. (Gloriana: You have some sauce here. D of H: I am very saucy. Gloriana, slapping him with her napkin: Oh, *you*.)

Meanwhile I do not want there to be allegiances that I am not part of. (For instance, when conversation briefly breaks the table in half, into three and two, I overhear Tom ask Mélanie how she would like to be 'embedded'. Hmm? With the troops, Tom hastens, and I know he is sweating. Ah. I would like it very much. While this little exchange is going on, I feel as if my clothes have been torn off on my right side, which is where Tom is sitting. I feel exposed and abandoned.)

Nonetheless, all these negotiations and shifting alliances leave me feeling pleasantly tired. I find I am losing track of time. I forget how far from home I have come. In the presence of the Dean of Humanity and his subjects, I am, however briefly, no longer waiting.

We are talking of war. It was bound to come up. Mélanie is spinning the globe, dropping us in all sorts of unfortunate places. She and Gloriana become even more animated. Gloriana stops the globe with her knife.

When Mélanie says the words 'crimes against humanity', it is inevitable that Tom and I look at the Dean.

What should we do with such men? Gloriana is asking.

The Hague has embarrassed itself with Milosevic, says Mélanie.

The Americans would execute everyone, says Gloriana.

What are your thoughts, Dean? asks Tom.

We all watch him. Mélanie puts down her fork. The Hague, he says, is a good place to start.

Yes, of course they must be sent to The Hague, says Gloriana impatiently. And then?

And then, blurts Mélanie, they should be forced to cohabitate. They should be made to endure each other's company.

Gloriana laughs. Yes.

The Dean smiles. Like Sartre's *Huis Clos*, he says.

Hell is other people, says Mélanie.

Sartre said that? I perk up.

In a play, says the Dean. *Huis Clos* or *No Exit*. Hell is a room shared by four people for all eternity.

You should read it, says Mélanie.

I think not, says the Dean. He winks at me. No one seems to notice.

It seems fitting, ventures Tom. I mean, that they should have to live together.

And what would be served by it? asks the Dean. You put a man who has committed atrocious acts with other men who have committed atrocious acts. At first they congratulate each other; then they commiserate; finally they try to outdo one another.

Let them, says Mélanie. In closed quarters, among themselves.

Tom presses the Dean: So what do you suggest?

The Dean rubs dry hands together. He considers. A man who has committed crimes against humanity should not be isolated from humanity. Nor should he be encouraged by others who have committed similar crimes. Let me give you a scenario. Every day the war criminal has a benevolent visitor. He and the visitor travel together to a place special or sacred to the visitor. There they spend the day together. At the end of that time, he is returned to his cell at The Hague, where the next day the process begins afresh, with a new visitor. This goes on indefinitely.

Sounds like a nice life, says Gloriana.

Why shouldn't it be nice? says the Dean.

Mélanie is horrified. Because he should *suffer* as he has made others suffer.

That is impossible. You know it is. And even if we could make him suffer as thousands, perhaps even *millions*, have suffered under him, we could not do so without *becoming* him. Do you see?

We are silent.

The Dean softens. Where would you take him, he asks his niece. Say you are the virtuous visitor.

Mélanie shakes her head. You cannot make me spend the day with a man who has committed genocide. She says this as if the Dean has really asked her to. As if it's pending. Tomorrow or the next day, the war criminal will arrive at the war correspondent's door, and off they will go to the zoo.

Perhaps you should reconsider your profession, says the Dean.

Silence.

I would take him to Niagara Falls, says Gloriana, standing to clear the plates.

Ha! says the Dean and the tension eases. But you've never been there. How is Niagara Falls sacred or special?

I've imagined it, says Gloriana dreamily, often enough. The honeymoon capital of the world.

You are going with a war criminal, Melanie reminds her.

You are perhaps starved for romance, my dear? says the Dean, reaching out to rub her elbow.

Perhaps, she says coyly and carries plates into the kitchen.

And you, Tom? Where would you take the war criminal?

So it has become a little game, and we will go around the table. It is in poor taste, maybe. I am getting some very strong poor-taste vibes from Mélanie.

Tom has to think about it. We wait. Gloriana returns. Coffee burbles in the kitchen.

Outer space? Gloriana offers helpfully, and again Tom regards her with a bewildered expression. Gloriana is apparently convinced that Tom's book is about space travel.

No, he says politely. I was thinking more along the lines of Hawaii. Maybe some snorkelling. Then we would golf.

I laugh, but the Dean lifts a finger and says, No, no. I am curious as to why this place and these activities?

Has anyone been to Kauai? Tom asks around the table. We all shake our heads.

Describe it, says Mélanie, a little bossily I think, but Tom doesn't seem to mind.

There are mountains like bunched-up green blankets. And a breeze always. It's never too hot. Under the water there are fish, iridescent, that kiss your fingers.

Lovely, says the Dean. And why take the war criminal there?

Because it's beautiful.

I'm a little embarrassed for our Writer in Residence. Surely he can do better than that?

And because, he stammers. Because it's gentle. Because golf is a gentle sport. And because, he adds, I might be afraid of such a man in any other place.

Such a man. Who are we each imagining?

Fair enough, says the Dean.

Surely the war criminal will be guarded, says Gloriana suddenly. For his own protection and ours. Otherwise, what's to stop him fleeing into those bunched-up green mountains?

The Dean looks at her a moment. Of course, he says. There will be guards.

Gloriana relaxes into her chair. In plain clothes, she says.

Fine.

We are interrupted by the doorbell. No one moves.

Well, we all know who that is, says the Dean finally, standing.

Not funny, Gloriana whispers.

We are like children who have been telling ghost stories. We are like Scrooge on Christmas Eve, only we are the ghosts, and it is something worse than Scrooge at the door.

Did someone order a cab? asks the Dean, stepping back into the dining room.

I sink in my chair. That would be me, I say. I didn't think it would actually show up.

When did you call a cab? asks Gloriana, confused.

Days ago.

What about you, Nicole? asks the Dean. He has sent the cab on its way.

Mélanie watches me disapprovingly.

Only my desk comes to mind, lit by a single lamp. But I can't say that. I cast about for somewhere more imaginative to take my war criminal. On the wall above my desk there is a *Desertscapes* calendar. This month's desert is the Mojave. The sun sets behind a yucca tree, black fingers spread in a gesture of goodbye. I concentrate very hard on this image and say, The Mojave Desert.

Is that in Arizona? asks Gloriana.

California. I continue to concentrate very hard on my calendar.

Why there? asks the Dean.

Because it's empty. I push my chair back a bit. What I mean is, it's not crowded. So we wouldn't be disturbed.

You and the war criminal? says the Dean.

Right, I say. I get the uneasy feeling he knows I'm describing a desk, not a desert.

You are not worried, Mélanie interrupts, that the presence of the war criminal will contaminate your special places?

Of all of us, she who has refused to play the game is taking it most seriously.

But this is all just hypothetical, says Gloriana gently.

No, it isn't, says Mélanie, her eyes on the Dean. The next time you think of Kauai, or Niagara Falls, or the Mojave Desert – you may find yourselves in the custody of a stranger.

I pick nervously at my wineglass and think about calling another cab.

You mean, Tom corrects her, with a stranger in *our* custody.

Mélanie shrugs.

Gloriana again mentions the presence of guards.

Yes, guards. Mélanie throws up her hands. So there will be a crowd.

Fortunately, says Gloriana, my place is already crowded.

The Dean chuckles. Niagara Falls is full of war criminals.

This isn't funny, says Mélanie.

She is not so brave after all, the war correspondent. I want to hold her hand across the table. Because I *am* brave. I can bring a stranger into my desert. Of course, my desert is not really a desert. It's just a picture on my wall. One of twelve. It really hasn't cost me anything to invite someone in.

It's your turn, says Gloriana to the Dean.

So it is. He leans forward, elbows on the table. I think, he says, we would just stay at The Hague.

Gloriana huffs. That's not a real answer.

But wait, says the Dean. We would stay in his cell and I would read to him.

Of course. A book. The most sacred space of all.

What would you read? I ask.

Sartre, Mélanie suggests.

The Dean shakes his head. I would read Tom's book.

We laugh, then feel badly about it.

Tom says, Seriously.

I am serious.

I don't believe you.

The Dean puts a hand on Tom's arm. My dear man, he says. Have you so little faith in your own gift? Why do you think I brought you here?

Gloriana brings coffee. We turn another page. We are happy, all of us, but particularly Tom.

Congratulations, I nudge him.

He gives me his bewildered look, but unsuccessfully this time. It's not every day the Dean of Humanity chooses to read your book to a war criminal. Tom can't hide that he's thrilled.

Even Mélanie is smiling. The table is clear. There are no forks left to pick up. She sips her coffee. Okay, she says. Bruges.

The Dean nods. Good choice.

I'm sorry? says Gloriana. You've lost me.

A town in Belgium, says Tom, who will never be lost again.

Near Flanders, says Mélanie. But Bruges, even more than Flanders, is a place of ghosts. Isn't that right, uncle?

Yes, you can feel the dead.

And there is a convent with a quadrangle at its centre, and in the quadrangle there are black trees that never sprout leaves and white doves on the branches. It is beautiful, and haunted.

Thank you, Mélanie, says the Dean.

And that is the end of that.

I feel like standing and making a speech. *I'd like to thank everyone who made tonight possible. Even Art Space and the hateful cab company.* But there is nothing on the table to use as a microphone, so instead I drink my coffee and listen to Gloriana describe last month's eclipse of the moon – how the moon turned pink in the shadow of the earth, and how that shadow is proof that we exist. We exist because we can make a pink shadow across the moon. There we are.

But I am only half listening. I am composing, in my head, the thank-you note I will write tomorrow. I will sit at my desk, beneath the Mojave Desert, and compose a letter that begins:

Dear Dean,

I wonder if you know that your niece refers to you as the Dean of Humanity? A title which, after last night, I find particularly fitting. . . .

The Anxiety Exhibit

Black Beauty is a child's story about a horse who passes through many hands, mostly hard and cruel. But you, little reader, know that when Black Beauty finds herself in hell, the next place she arrives will be bliss. And you know too, that just when she finds herself in a warmly lit stable, stroked by gentle fingers, a good whipping waits around the next corner.

Justine is a story by the Marquis de Sade about a French girl who passes through many hands, mostly hard and cruel. But you, little reader, know that when Justine finds herself in hell, the next place she arrives will be bliss. And you know too, that just when she finds herself safe and sleepy in a warm bed, a libertine's footsteps will be heard on the stairs (make that several libertines' footsteps), and she will be dragged by the hair to the dungeon where torture such as you have never imagined awaits her.

Your first boyfriend's front door is painted white badly with congealed drips of paint you can pick off with your thumbnail if you are left waiting too long. You are twelve years old. You drop by around 4:00 p.m. and are admitted to the basement where Joey's brother has a waterbed. The brother lives in the basement (because he's a libertine?) because it's the only floor in the badly built house that supports the weight of the bed. The brother works in the afternoons, so you and Joey have the basement to yourselves.

It is dark, as basements tend to be, lit only by an aquarium in which three piranhas (yes, the kind that will eat you alive and leave only your bones!) swim in front of three girls' naked bums. The naked bums are lit up. The source of the light comes from somewhere behind the naked bums. The piranhas swim in front of this picture without looking at it.

If you don't kiss me, Joey says, I'll put your hand in the aquarium.

Sometimes he pushes you down, sort of rough, and there is a rubbery splash, a contained splash that is not allowed to be, followed by angry waves. The bed asks to be let loose in the room. Both you and Joey sense this, but have no language for it.

Instead Joey says, Imagine the waterbed leaked, and the room filled up with water and tipped over the aquarium, and the fish swam into the room and ate us in our sleep.

Jeeze, Joey. I'd never fall asleep down here.

Me either.

You don't like kissing Joey. Sloppy are his lips. Sloppy is the bed. But the piranhas look hungry, and do you really have a choice?

Your favourite movie is about a boy and a horse who are shipwrecked on a desert island. The horse has passed through many hands, mostly hard and cruel, but guess what? That's all over now. Now there is just the boy and the horse and the story of the boy winning the horse's trust. Most of the movie is quiet. Desert islands are quiet. When the boy and the horse are rescued, you are filled with anxiety. How can such a little boy keep such a huge animal safe in the world? You continue to worry long after the movie stops.

Your second boyfriend's front door is wood and allowed to look like wood. It even smells like wood. It has a stained-glass window, and in the winter at around 4:00 p.m. when you drop by, the entranceway is a kaleidoscope pointed at the sun.

The den has thirteen-foot ceilings. It gets dark as soon as Andrew wants it to. The windows, which bulge outward like eyes, turn to blank silver, ice-crusted around the edges. The stereo in the corner winks like a distant city.

You and Andrew hunker down on the sofa and listen to Billy Ocean sing 'Caribbean Queen'. Andrew has been to the Caribbean. You think of the girls' bums in Joey's brother's aquarium. There was some sand on those bums. Just a few specks. They were likely on a beach, those bums, in the Caribbean.

You and Andrew make out. You pretend you're on a beach. Your toes point at an ocean brighter than stained glass. You are tanned as you've never been tanned before. Even your bum is tanned.

Andrew's tongue moves inside your mouth like a cat drinking. He adopts the precise rhythm of Mitsy at her water bowl. This is wrong, and unpleasant.

The exhibit is called Anxiety. On a white pedestal a goldfish swims in a fishbowl. The sign underneath reads:

Fleur Blanchette carried this fish on her person for 365 days, usually in a sealed plastic bag. During that year, she worked part-time at Kinko's and completed an undergraduate degree in History. 'My goal,' says the artist, 'was to see if I could carry something with me forever – in the shower, in my sleep, to never put it down or let it go, to keep it alive and avoid damaging it.'

You watch the fish swim on its pedestal at the heart of the Art Gallery of Ontario. You are the only one in the room. It's Christmas Eve. The gallery will be closing soon. Your heart lurches. How could Fleur Blanchette leave the fish here, alone? Where is she? And is she anxious?

The front door of your third boyfriend's house has three tear-shaped windows. The tears get larger as they descend. A front door crying. You drop by after school. You are admitted, and directly you're on the threshold of the living room. There is no transition space here. A closet for your coat, a mat for your boots, and the deep carpet is already beginning under your feet.

You follow Sean to his room in the basement. Yes, another basement. But this room belongs to him (he has no brothers), and he has a regular bed. He also has a little bright lamp on a desk that is not really a desk but several stacked bricks with a front door between them. The front door that is his desk is the twin of the real front door upstairs. On this desk he builds model airplanes and little model soldiers of the World War Two era. He confesses that he pretends the tear-shaped windows are bodies of water.

You like Sean a lot. But you have learned a thing or two. You have a story for Sean. You've been in two abusive relationships, you tell him. You've been forced to do things that made you uncomfortable. Joey pushed you around and threatened your life with piranhas. Andrew wouldn't take no for answer and slurped like a cat. Now you are afraid of intimacy, you tell him.

You have an inkling that Sean will like this story, and he does. It's not that he's sadistic or a libertine – but Sean wants to be different from those who came before him.

Sean is a hero. He says, I'd never make you do anything you didn't want to.

You pick up a model soldier and drop him at the centre of a tear-shaped lake. Really?

At a party when you are seventeen a girl you barely know asks you to come home with her to protect her from her father, who is a libertine. You say no. She is lying. You are so sure she is lying because you have lied yourself. What a drama queen, you think, and leave her to wait for a cab in the snow by herself.

Troilus and Cressida is a play about a woman who passes through many hands, mostly hard and cruel, Trojan and Greek. You in the audience know that when Troilus is true he is lying, and when Cressida is false she is also lying, and there is nothing to be done about it except to count the iterations on the stage.

You are alone at the AGO on Christmas Eve because you have left your boyfriend and you are staying in a hotel not far from the gallery.

The front door of the house you shared with your thirty-first boyfriend had a bevelled window that broke the street into slabs. When the cab came to take you away, you saw it through this window first, and hesitated. But then you were outside, and all the edges connected, and you were leaving.

You left your thirty-first boyfriend in the house you shared for two years, sitting at the kitchen table, staring at one of the placemats that is a map of the world. You left him memorizing, perhaps, the capital of Burkina Faso, which is Ouagadougou, and which is the one, when you quizzed him, that he always got wrong.

This is a story about you, reader, who have passed through many hands, none of which were particularly hard or cruel, but from which you plotted your escape anyway. Because just when you come to the heart of the story, a new one (that is really the same one) is beginning elsewhere, and you must hurry if you are going to make your entrance at the appointed time.

You have wondered, on occasion, how many iterations are enough?

One Person Speaks the Truth

To protect or be protected.

This was the question he put to the group. Quieted us right down, I can tell you. All three tables. As if he'd unleashed a big cat, right there in the restaurant. We sat, very still. We sat, very thrilled. Oh, nobody answer. Wait. Let the question dance a moment.

I closed my eyes. Pretend it's a UFO just spotted. Pretend it's your fortune, about to be read. Pretend it might actually matter.

Somebody said, It's the old murderer versus murderee question, isn't it?

No, said the man with the question. Murder has nothing to do with protection.

Ever?

Someone else said, It's a question of chivalry. For or against.

Oh, well – cough. Against. Too easy.

It wouldn't do to speak the truth. It wouldn't do to say: Save me.

So we all in the end agreed that protection, whether issued or received, is bad news.

But if I were the one to speak the truth, I would say, Listen. Listen to my fantasy. A man comes through that door with a semi-automatic weapon. You all crawl under the table, while I push back my chair. One swift ninja kick and I dislodge the weapon, send it twirling, catch it like a baton in my open hands. I turn it on him. I say, Back up, real slow there, friend. What's this all about? Go home to your wife and kids.

And he does.

Then, on my way home, I rescue the man with the question from a runaway train. It's skidding down the street at a forty-five-degree angle. It's taking out the buildings on either side. It's scraping the street clean. We're on foot, the man with the question and I. He says, We're dead. But I say no. I pull him into an alley. We run between two brick walls, our hands clasped. When I deem it safe, we stop. He presses his back against the brick. I press my chest against his. We are breathing heavy, but he is breathing heavier than me. I kiss him, but not for as long as he'd like. Then we finish the walk home.

But not before we stumble upon a downed electrical wire (likely a far-reaching effect of the train derailment), dancing like a snake, spitting venomous light. The man with the question, charmed, is moving in. I grab his collar. What are you doing? It's a live wire.

It's beautiful, he says.

But it's really just the magnetic field – and I tell him so – reeling him in. That's why they keep such wires over our heads or under the ground. Because we'd be touching them all the time. Reaching out for death.

I ask him, What would you do without me? I can't count how many pianos have fallen from the sky, have grazed your shoulders without you noticing.

Or the number of thugs who have stalked you, who have wanted you dead. Lucky for you I carry a weapon under my dress.

This is the goddamn truth. But I say nothing.

The person next to me, Sheila, says, I like your blue nail polish.

Once in a dream I had a boil on my inner thigh. A huge pus-filled business. I popped it and my thigh split open lengthwise, a deep wedge in the flesh. What emerged wasn't pus after all, but an ancient dagger. Ornate. Deadly.

There has been nothing, in my waking or sleeping life, so satisfying as yanking that dagger from my leg and seeing the hole it left behind.

This is another thing it would not do to say aloud, here, now, at the dinner table.

I do, however, take a deep breath and reply to Sheila: I've painted my nails blue since I was eighteen. I had a crush on a girl who always had at least one blackened fingernail. Sometimes two or three. She built things, you see – difficult and extraordinary things that damaged her hands. For three summers we worked together at a camp in

Wisconsin. I was art. She was woodworking. I learned there is nothing sexier than damaged fingers. But I was a soak-in-Palmolive kind of girl. I didn't have the balls to let loose on my own hands with a hammer and achieve an authentic damaged finger of my own. So I opted for painting my nails blue. I can still glance down at my hands and see hers.

This is what I have left.

Vanda fell out of the cart, right in front of my eyes. Two tires ran over her stomach, thump, thump. I turned around and she was lying in the gravel road. How many of us were in that cart? Twelve? Twelve times an average of 150 pounds. What is that? Plus the cart itself, and the few remaining duffel bags we were delivering to the cabins.

Vanda in the road, and me springing out and running back, to be intercepted by John and Jason, EMTs in a previous life. They knew what to do. Don't crowd her, they said.

And because I was not allowed to protect, I needed protection. Because I was not allowed to protect, I collapsed in the gravel road, thirty feet away, until someone came and collected me.

She lasted a week. My weight in the cart was part of her death.

Vanda of the blue-black nails. Vanda: For you, I carry a dagger. For you, I paint my nails to match the sapphires in the hilt.

In one of my fantasies, I tell Sheila, I'm out for my early morning walk. I pass a parked car, and I hear thump, thump – coming from the trunk.

Save me.

Are you locked in?

What does it look like?

Wait there. I'll go call the police.

I run home, thinking: Of course she'll wait. Where else is she going to go? My feet fly.

I tell the police, I'll be waiting by the car. Please hurry.

I run back to the car and place a warm hand on the trunk. I crouch down, dare to say her name. Vanda? The police are coming.

Thank you.

You're welcome.

Two cars arrive, lights flashing but no sirens. The neighbourhood is still asleep. These are considerate cops.

They use a special doo-hickey to spring the trunk.

And there is Vanda, alive, wrists and ankles bound. The police lean in to untie her, but I clear my throat, and they let me do the honours.

I hold her hand as she steps out of the trunk. She collapses into my arms. I breathe into her hair. I say, It's okay. I'm here. I'm here.

This is my favourite fantasy. It ends with her slamming the trunk down on my four fingers. An accident. She puts them in her mouth. She says, I'm sorry. Don't cry. Don't cry.

And do you? Sheila asks.

It varies, I say. Sometimes I do, sometimes I don't.

Engineers

The Engineering building had rooms you could lie down in. Rooms that got dark, doors that locked. And best of all, carpet that didn't chafe your ass – a luxury after what passed for carpet in my mother's office. Which is where we started that winter, where it all started.

Saturday nights I would race to the heated overpass, stolen keys inside my mitten. Greg would be waiting on a concrete step.

Come on.

In the dark of my mother's office, I would sit in the teacher's chair, he in the bad-student chair. I would cross my legs. I would say, If only you applied yourself. Or, You're failing. While he leaned over and kissed me, pulled me down onto orange Velcro.

You're failing, I repeated.

You're *falling*, he said.

Yeah. In love.

Knees, palms, elbows, and asses rubbed raw by spring.

That year, spring sprang a nightmare called Double Daylight Savings Time. All Newfoundland clocks went ahead two hours instead of one. The government was manufacturing daylight.

My mother's dirty windows let in all the double daylight and then some. Her office was on the ground floor. Anyone might walk by.

We explored other venues.

We crossed the overpass to the site of the new Earth Sciences building. It was just steel and concrete then, open to the un-darkening sky. We camped out in a construction shack, the door wired shut, the windows blacked out with garbage bags. For a few weeks, we manufactured darkness. Then a padlock appeared on the door.

We travelled further afield. The Geology Department had a trailer down by Long Pond. Greg shimmied in through a hatch at the back and welcomed me through the front door. Come in, come in.

Why, thank you.

The curtains were orange, a cross between cotton and cardboard. They kept out the light.

What do Geology people do? I asked, opening all the miniature cupboards.

Geologists, he said, collect the earth.

But I found no evidence of the earth. No footprints. No rocks with frozen pictures. No leaves, bark, grass. The place was immaculate. We were careful to leave it that way.

Someone caught on nonetheless. We arrived one night to find a note on the front door: *No Skin Tonight*. Greg tore it down, said nothing. And that night, there wasn't any. Skin. That night, he wouldn't touch me.

One very bright night we stumbled into the Engineering building and discovered some very dark rooms. We locked a door and waited for our eyes to adjust. They didn't. Perfect, I said.

The carpet was living-room thick. They're rich on this side of the overpass, I said.

On our backs in the dark, Greg said, Why did they take away the night?

So there'd be no skin. I turned. My lips touched his bare shoulder. No skin tonight.

He moaned.

He had a curfew. I did not. The sun was barely setting at midnight.

Don't go, I would say, every time. Don't go yet. Hooking my fingers over his collar bone.

But he would. He was good. We pulled our pants on in the dark. Outside we squinted.

The front of the lecture theatre felt like a stage. Hundreds of empty chairs faced us in the dark.

What do Engineering people do? I asked.

Engineers, he said, drive trains.

So people come here to learn to drive trains?

Yup.

We flicked a switch. I drew a train on the blackboard, under a spotlight. I gave the train 12 cars and a caboose. Underneath I wrote: Go Engineers!

My new walkman had two outlets for earphones. He had a pair; I had a pair. We faced each other on the carpet and shared what we loved.

Listen to this song.

Listen to this song.

Kiss me to this song.

I wanted to go all the way. If I get pregnant, I said, I'll have an abortion. No big whoop.

I have a leather jacket like Madonna in the 'Papa Don't Preach' video. I walk the way she walks, along the railroad tracks.

The Engineers pass by in their trains. I look deep into their eyes. They fall in love with me by the thousands. The Engineers. They dream of me from their conductors' chairs.

One day I lie across the tracks. The train stops just in time. Out leaps an Engineer. He pulls me up by the wrists. He takes me into his train. He sits me down in his conductor's chair. He kneels. He says, Don't ever do that again. He kisses me. He pulls me down onto the train floor.

This was the story I told myself, over and over, during the summer of double daylight.

I acted it out when my parents weren't home. I walked up and down the driveway like Madonna. I lay on the tracks (my father's ladder). I went inside for the kissing scenes. The statue of Mary on the landing was a little shorter than me. That's why my Engineer was always kneeling.

We're too young for sex, Greg said for the hundredth time.

We're not too young for other things. Like blow jobs.

He was quick to point out that blow jobs carry no risk.

What about my jaw?

The first time, in my mother's office, my jaw had locked open. He'd had to massage my face in the dark until I calmed down, until my mouth closed.

What if I'd had to go home and explain that? I said. Imagine that.

You couldn't have, he said, if your mouth was locked open.

Very funny.

You were scared, he said. That's why it happened. I'm sorry.

Don't be sorry.

I was thinking: You can bet Madonna's jaw never locked open.

Greg said, Next year, it'll be Triple Daylight Savings Time. I've heard talk.

They can't do that.

Sure they can. They're just getting started.

The night will still come, I said, no matter what. They can't do the Triple. The rest of the world won't let them. They barely let them do this.

We sat at a large mahogany table in a conference room, the lights dimmed. Between us, on the table, a large crucified Jesus pointed his ballet feet at me.

How'd you get in? I asked.

Through the front door.

Nobody stopped you.

No.

He'd just walked into his old homeroom, stood on the teacher's desk, and lifted the crucifix from the wall over the blackboard.

Close up like this, Jesus looked like he was dancing, like he was leaping. A cross just happened to be attached to his back, but he could handle it – look at those muscles!

I peered at the initials over his head. What does INRI stand for?

I'm Nailed Right In.

Go on.

Greg propped Jesus over the blackboard in the conference room. The Engineers need a little Jesus, he said.

And I could see that. Trains sometimes come off their tracks.

Before turning out the lights, we swivelled in our chairs and admired the effect.

I think it's INR*L*, I said.

Yeah? For what?

For I Never Really Lived.

There are no trains in Newfoundland, I told him one night in the lecture theatre. I asked my parents.

He faced away from me. Typical, he said.

Do you think the Engineers know?

They're not stupid.

Maybe they're hoping the trains will come back. Maybe this is all just in case.

No, he said. They'll leave. They'll go where the trains are. There are trains everywhere but here.

Oh.

And there was night everywhere but here too. Long, dark summer nights.

We left the earphones in, which limited movement, but it was worth it for the soundtrack. I let Greg pick the music.

He said, It may never be this dark again.

Right, I said. This is as dark as it gets.

We went all the way. It felt the same as everything else. Afterwards I asked him, Are you sure we haven't done that before?

I'm sure.

Only the lecture theatre felt different. The chairs didn't seem so empty. It felt like we'd been found out.

And then we were.

The door on one side of the theatre opened. A plank of double daylight cut through the dark.

A voice said, For the love of Christ.

Lights came on.

Get dressed. The security guard stood in the aisle, his face averted.

Greg's pants were on and he was up before I'd even found my underwear. I was not going to hurry.

How old are you?

None of your business, I said.

Greg told him.

Jesus.

I did up my jeans. How old are *you*, old man?

He pointed a finger at me. You. Shut your mouth.

Greg said nothing.

So it's been you two all along. Been all over the map, haven't you?

Yup.

Aren't you the brazen one.

We walked up the aisle, past him. Touch me and die, I said.

Believe me, miss. You don't have to worry.

Now, in a lecture on statics and dynamics, I turn to the boy next to me and say: I lost my virginity in this room.

His pen stops.

Back when I thought engineers drove trains, I say. Before I knew there were other kinds of engineers. Can you imagine? I laugh. This has only now occurred to me.

I'm sorry, he says.

But he has misunderstood. He thinks I'm telling a different kind of story. Oh, no. I put a hand on his shoulder. No. It's funny, don't you think?

George the Third Wasn't Mad Forever.
(He Got Better, and So Might I.)

I break off the inner chant to remind myself: You're not mad.
There is a way back to the eighteenth century. Here is the recipe:

Step 1: Fall out of love with people you know.
Step 2: Fall in love with people you don't.
Step 3: Fall in love with people who have just died –
then work your way back to people who died longer
ago and longer ago, until you reach the year you
want to return to.
Step 4: Cry on television.

Then you'll be gone.

I'm on step 3.

Thomas Chatterton died in 1770. He was seventeen. A poet and
imposter – he forged hundreds of medieval manuscripts. This is how
it's done: Age the parchment with ochre. Perfect your Gothic script.
Change 'i' to 'y'; double up your consonants; add 'e' to the ends of
words. Step on the parchment. Crumple. Apply more ochre. And
voila! Ancient poetry.

People bought it. When they stopped buying it, Thomas Chatterton took arsenic. But I'm not in love with Thomas Chatterton. Not
yet. I'm in love with Meyerstein, his biographer. A twentieth-century
biographer, but dead. In 1929 he completed *A Life of Thomas Chatterton*. He had returned from World War I and wanted to get back to the
eighteenth century. I think he succeeded. I'm sure he did. He was able
to fall in love with Chatterton. He completed step 3.

He really was in love with the boy.

THIS IMPERFECT ESSAY

IS DEDICATED

TO ITS SUBJECT

IN HUMBLE CONSCIOUSNESS

THAT I HAVE NOT BEEN UNJUST

TO THE MEMORY OF

AN ENGLISH POET

There I was, watching the shadow-puppet life of Thomas Chatterton unfold on the cave wall, when I saw the dedication, scratched into the stone. And I turned around – slowly, so as not to scare the biographer, slowly, to see him dancing before the fire. He was dancing out the poet's life, in flames and shadows – for me. And for that, I loved him.

Meyerstein has been dead since, or gone since, step 4. Obviously. It's doubtful he cried on television, though not impossible. Say he died in the fifties or sixties.

But before television, any public event would do, I imagine. What you need is the emotional catharsis and the witnesses, the wading back through Romanticism and coming out on the other side, intact. Then, like I said, you'll be gone.

I started by stopping loving my husband. It was sufficient I found to like him a lot. Only in the very early mornings, seeing him off at the airport, would I feel sick and deprived. He left me under the clouds – while up there, I knew, the cabin was the color of Tang, the flight attendants made up like nighttime. On those mornings, the airport was a lightless, loveless place.

Then he didn't return from one of his consulting trips. Problem solved. The last thing he consulted me on was my name. He said, Take your first name, Ann, and your second, Marie, and push them up against each other, make them one word, and leave the M capital like a support beam in the middle. That's what all the businesses are doing.

That's the first thing I tell them to do. Then I add a dot com and voila. AnnMarie Dot Com. AnnMarie Meyerstein. AnneMarrye Meyerstteyne.

It occurs to me now that Chatterton was trying to get back to the fifteenth century. No doubt the poems, maps, coats of arms and all the rest of the supporting documentation he created were part of the recipe for getting back to the Renaissance. A more complicated procedure than mine. I'm glad that's not where I want to go.

I see him running through the streets of London, screaming: The Romantics are coming, the Romantics are coming. And they were coming all right – for *him*. Blake, that psychopath, at the fore – marching back with handcuffs, seeking out the wrists of the poor boy poet, the tragic genius. Oh the Romantics wanted him *bad*.

But Chatterton knew they were coming. He followed the steps. Then he was gone.

The fraud is most evident in the Christmas tree. The way it becomes furniture after a week. And you have to add more bulbs and make the room dark just to suck a little magic from the branches. Then that too fades to black. No matter how gorgeous – pretty soon you won't see it. And you'll be looking through that same tiny hole, down at your own feet, or at the numbers on the microwave.

So you add Handel's *Messiah*. You progress to giant Christmas rock ballads. You buy a menorah. You pray. You walk from room to room and think – Jesus, I'm half starved.

Because it's just you and your body and this fraud perpetrated by the Romantics. The only way out is step 4.

You haven't lived until you've cried on television.

Preferably it will happen as a result of some terrifically moving experience – a blessing from the Pope, a gold medal in women's figure skating. But I'd settle for witnessing somebody else's tragedy.

JP2, we love you. That's what they were chanting at the Pope's mass, their faces wet with tears. I could do that.

Or, clutching my roses, puffing and lovely: Yes, it was my first quad. I never thought I'd pull it off.

Or, floating aboard a piece of fuselage. Just me on a scrap of wing. I was saved while 103 went down.

I will cry on TV. And the world will cry with me.

I'm not saying that my elation/grief won't be real. Well, yes, I am saying that. It won't be. But my desire to cry on television – my relief at having finally achieved it – that will be real. You'll know it when you see it. Here is a life's goal fulfilled, you'll say. Here is an end to the longing.

My husband bought us a house on a giant lake. I've seen cities, past and future, on the other side. It's a trick of the eye, I know. The temperature, the humidity, the refraction of light – it all combines to build up the air into something remarkably believable.

There was a holy city one night, pointy and treacherous. There was a city on stilts – and the next night, a city that no longer needed them – it had learned how to float. There was a city of steel, full of fire and industry.

I've seen the Batman symbol in the sky overhead.

And once, at dusk, I saw a city of roller coasters. The most frighteningly elaborate double helixes you've ever seen – the DNA of God himself – pressed against a sunset. You can make a city out of anything.

But you know the one I'm waiting for.

The temptation is still there. To get a little love. There is love to be had, you find yourself thinking.

Twice I've faltered. It's a game of Snakes and Ladders. You could be up to step 3, land on a snake, and whoa Jesus – you're back loving people you know, from this century, this decade, this very year.

Most recently it was my high-school sweetheart. He asked me to dinner. Over the phone I warned him: My husband's gone. I'm shut down for the winter. There's no thaw a-comin'. Catch my drift? He said, Remember the sex we used to have?

In fact, I was in no danger. From the moment he pitied me at the restaurant, I was in no danger. He sat down across from me and saw that 85 percent of me was already dead.

He said, When was the last time you masturbated? Adding: And enjoyed it?

And what do you say to something like that? Oh. And *enjoyed it*. Well, that changes everything because –

There were people at the other tables who overheard. That was fine. I was fine with that. We could do a little *When Harry Met Sally* routine if that's what he wanted.

I said: I don't remember. The truth. And his response: That breaks my heart.

And I'll talk about masturbation over a megaphone – bring one to the table – but Christ, don't pity me – don't make all these people visualize me *not* masturbating.

Understand, I said by way of explanation, to him and to everyone, I've been asleep for years.

And across from me, he was picking up the gauntlet. I could awaken you, he said.

No, no you couldn't. I wanted to smoosh his face into the bread basket and tell him I'd already been woken, albeit briefly, by someone else. Oh yes. Someone else. Not him.

This was the other time I spoke of, when I nearly slipped back to step 1. Unlike the high-school sweetheart, this was a very close call.

A wedding. I was seated at the young and unmarried table – because I'm sort of unmarried now, I guess, and still not un-young. And beside me was a man with a cynicism and humour that reminded me of – what else? – my favourite century. We snickered into our salmon – the bride and groom's initials were seared onto the pink flesh. During the toasts, we laughed in all the wrong places. I was in a very good mood; I was in very great danger. Then we saw the baby. He said, Look at that baby. So I did. And the baby looked at him. And he looked at me. We made this triangle – and I thought: Are such things possible? I was in very great danger.

Eighty-five percent of me is dead, I said, but he didn't hear. I don't think such words were in his vocabulary. Words like *eighty-five percent* and *dead*.

Look at that baby – those were in his vocabulary.

So I let myself imagine: The two of us in a grocery store, our arms linked. He is very tall, and I stand on my tiptoes to kiss his unshaven cheek. I feel no repulsion whatsoever. Everything but him fades to black. All the food – we can't see it. It can rot. It won't be eaten. The garbage trucks will have to come and take it away. It's not our responsibility. The future. It simply isn't.

Had he felt what I felt – it would have been back to step 1 for me. But he didn't. True to my favourite century, he didn't indulge me. The humour and cynicism had been for their own sake, not for mine. He was my true love. I know because he didn't love me. I ate the initials, looked up, and he was gone.

I'm in the middle of the giant lake because I've finally seen it – an eighteenth-century city on the other side. I've completed step 3, paid my respects to Meyerstein – moved on, moved back, to George the Third. It was George the Third all along, of course. He is so easy to love. I've been chanting about him for years. George the Third wasn't mad forever. He got better. Had he been born a century later, he wouldn't have.

I'm bypassing step 4. Dangerous – but I saw the city. And how could I not swim for it?

Only I'm dead weight. Eighty-five percent dead weight.

Back on the other side, lights are flashing. Crowds are gathering. They know I'm out here, drowning. They must have sent the dog. Because here he is beside me, a golden retriever. And is he ever golden. A little piece of sun, treading black water. He's here to retrieve me. That's his job. Okay, I say.

On the beach, someone wraps me and holds me and tells me I'm all bone. No wonder I didn't float.

But I was so close.

There is an ambulance, and beside it, two vans with wires and antennas. The local news. They are speaking to my husband. Where did he come from? He's been gone for years.

She would have died, he is saying, if not for Bounder.

A chorus of people ask him how he feels.

Who the hell is Bounder? Then I see it must be the dog – because my husband is staring down at the retriever, his face wet with tears.

Not so fast.

I am crumpled on the beach in a blanket, a compelling and pathetic sight. Bounder, I call, coughing up water. Come here, baby. And the well-named dog bounds up to me. The reporters and cameras follow.

My husband is yesterday's news.

Della Renfrew

My mother and I, in search of the underground Science Shop, entered through Holt Renfrew. It was a Saturday. The winter sun was low in the sky. We stepped into Holt's and the light was something brighter than halogen.

I paused, big as an astronaut in my winter coat. God, I said. How do you get a job at Holt Renfrew? How do you ever become crisp enough?

The women behind the counters wore interesting glasses. They were of a higher resolution than me.

Mum was making for the escalator. Somewhere below us, in the underground concourse, she would find an up-to-date globe.

Wait, I said.

Della, she warned. The rubber rail moved under her hand. She was about to step on. But I shook my head.

I knocked on the counter. Right. I'd like to apply for a job.

There were many women to choose from. But the one I'd selected had skin the colour of the room – concentrated white – so that she was just disembodied nostrils, interesting glasses, and red, unlicked lips.

She did not smile. She glanced right to left like a bad actress. Maybe she was hoping for backup. None came.

That's right, I said. Me. Job. Holt Renfrew.

I'm not sure that we're hiring, she said, her voice an amplified whisper.

I'll fill out an application anyway, I whispered back.

Her nostrils flared. Then, keeping her eyes on me, she sank down behind the counter. I removed my astronaut coat and looked around for my mother. No sign of her. I let the coat drop to the floor. It retained my shape.

An application was reluctantly produced.

So there really is such a thing, I said, rubbing my hands together. Whaddya know. Better give me some extra paper.

Disembodied frowned. She pulled some loose pages from a drawer. Maybe you'd like to take it home?

That won't be necessary. I'll fill it out right here.

She slid a pen across the counter. I'll be around the corner if you need me, she said.

Great.

In the space for my name, I wrote, Della Renfrew. Ha! See what they make of that.

The first question was, *Have you ever had a blemish? If so, when?*

Well, that's an easy one. Funny you should ask, I wrote. My most recent blemish was just this morning. One of those in-the-eyebrow variety – so easily hideable. I hope my having eyebrows doesn't prohibit me working here?

2. *Please describe your work experience, beginning with your current or most recent job.*

I am currently employed as a *liaison*. Due to the sensitive nature of my responsibilities, I am not at liberty to discuss the details.

Prior to becoming a *liaison*, I was simply the child of Holt Renfrew.

3. *Why do you want to work at Holt Renfrew?*

I have never been close to my father.

4. *Do you consider yourself a hairy person?*

Yes.

5. *Please describe your relationship history, beginning with your current or most recent love interest. In the space provided, explain why the past relationships failed.*

April 2003 to present: Lee van Rossum

Like me, Lee van Rossum is a *liaison*. He is ten years my junior and fairly new to the trade. We met last spring at a conference for *liaisons*. What Lee lacks in experience, he makes up for in personal style. He is always impeccably dressed. In fact, he shops here, on a different floor.

Lee's only flaw is his penchant for the word 'perhaps'. Indeed, it may become a point of contention, though I'm trying to be optimistic. According to the dictionary, 'perhaps' and 'maybe' are synonyms, but those of us in the business know better. No word is closer to a *liaison's* heart than 'maybe' (or in Lee's case, 'perhaps'). And while I completely endorse the use of the work-related 'perhaps', I'm not so fond of it in informal conversations with my loved one.

Me: Do you think traffic will be bad?

Lee: *Perhaps.*

Me: Is that tornado heading straight for us?

Lee: *Perhaps.*

I've tried subtle hints. Remarkably, Lee seems impervious. I say remarkably because the subtle hint is one of my specialties. The most effective subtle hint is the highly symbolic dream. Simply begin, 'I had the strangest dream last night', and proceed from there.

The dream I invented for Lee went like this: I had the strangest dream last night. I looked up the word 'annoying' in the dictionary, and the definition was 'perhaps'. I looked up other words – 'aggravating', 'irksome', 'pompous' – and all the definitions were the same: 'perhaps'.

What do you think that means? I asked Lee.

He shook his head. That is a pretty strange dream, he said.

1998–2000: Basil Stopes

I should probably explain the three-year gap between Basil Stopes and Lee van Rossum. It's been said that I have discerning taste in men. This is true. But my high standards (and the failure of most men to meet them) were unfortunately not the cause of this particular dry spell. Probably you've already guessed that Basil is dead. Thus the period of mourning. Approximately three years.

Basil was not a *liaison*. Basil was a choreographer. Sometimes he was difficult to be around. Patience was not Basil's middle name.

The only time I accompanied him on one of his 'tours', our luggage was lost. Delayed! the airline representative corrected. Not to worry. Our bags would be delivered to the hotel as soon as they arrived. We were given a tracking number and an 800 number to call.

Basil called that number incessantly. It was the very first thing he did when we checked into our room, and he didn't let up for three days. Most of the time – and this contributed to the mania – there was no answer. He would count the rings out loud to me. Twenty-three rings! Twenty-four rings! Holding the receiver away from his ear in disbelief. When he finally did get through, an automated voice asked him for the tracking number, and, when he punched it in, the voice laughed. So Basil said. I never called the number myself.

I began to wonder what was in those goddamn bags. Had they contained fifty kilos of heroin or a small arsenal, I might have forgiven his compulsive behaviour. But when the bags finally did arrive, there was nothing in them but the usual suspects: underwear, electric toothbrush, 'choreography' notes.

Over breakfast one morning, Basil told me his theory. Where do you think that 1-800-344-3602 number goes? he asked.

Goes? I tried not to be annoyed that he could recite the number by heart.

Where do you think it actually rings?

Oh. I don't know. The airport? The airline?

He laughed – and although I'd never heard it, I felt pretty sure he was imitating the laugh of the automated voice.

Okay, I said. Where?

An empty warehouse in New Jersey. There's a black phone on the floor. That's it.

Ah.

And it just rings.

Right, I said. And the automated voice?

God.

Poor Basil. I shook my head. But three weeks later, when he was dead, I considered that perhaps God really had been laughing at him, at his 'choreography', at his lost baggage, and I thanked my lucky stars I'd never called the number myself. I thanked my lucky stars I was a *liaison*. And I cried for Basil, of course. No one should be the victim of his own stage set. But you'd be surprised at how often this happens. The number of letters I've received since, from others who have lost choreographers in similar accidents, it just boggles the mind.

1997–1998: Bryan Macready

Bryan Macready was tragic for the first five minutes of *every single* day. This I could not abide. We lasted less than a year.

Get *up* for the love of Christ.

Tears in his eyes.

It's not that bad.

You have no idea.

Yes, I do. It's goddamn contagious. You make me want to kill you. Get in the shower.

This sounds harsh. But it was necessary.

It was as if all the little moments of semi-sadness that others feel over the course of a day were, for Bryan, concentrated into this moment of waking. As soon as he stepped into the shower, he was cured. He never once emerged from the bathroom the same pathetic creature who went in. But those five pre-shower minutes in the bedroom were unendurable.

One morning, I sat on the edge of the bed and tried not to pinch him. I said, I had the strangest dream last night. You were in it.

Bryan pulled the blankets up under his chin. Really?

I dreamt you were that guy in the Viagra commercial. You know the one who wakes up, *jumps* out of bed, and dances all over the house singing 'Good morning, good morning – it's *great* to stay up late!' You were doing these crazy acrobatics. It was wild.

I patted his leg gently with my open hand. I did not pinch him.

That doesn't sound like me, Bryan said meekly.

Nope. It sure doesn't.

The application was endless.

6. *How would you describe your relationship with your mother?*

There was a place below for her signature and the date. I knocked on the counter and summoned Disembodied.

Is my mother's signature really necessary here?

She turned the application towards her and studied it for a long time. I suspected she was reading about my relationship with Bryan Macready. I coughed.

Yes, she said finally.

Even if I'm well over eighteen?

She pushed the application back across the counter. We don't hire people under eighteen.

What if my mother was dead?

We don't hire people whose mothers are dead.

No, of course you don't.

Look, Ms. – she twisted her swan's neck to read the top of my application – Ms. *Renfrew*. Would you like to complete the application at home? Where your mother can sign it?

No. I'll finish it here. But I think you should know, I find this question about my mother intrusive.

She shrugged. Frankly, I agree with you. But we all had to fill it out. And why should you, Ms. *Renfrew*, be any different? She arched a missing eyebrow.

Just what are you implying?

Disembodied said nothing. For a moment I saw myself in her interesting glasses. Oversized pores. A forest of eyebrow. She turned away. I'll be around the corner if you need me, she said.

My coat pressed against my leg. I looked down. Not quite so pouffy now, are you?

I returned to the application.

6. How would you describe your relationship with your mother?

My mother and I go way back, I began, then crossed that out.

The first time I heard my mother use the word 'fuck', it was in the same sentence as the word 'Santa'. It was five in the morning. She was on the toilet. I was going to be a gingerbread man in the Santa Claus parade. I was already in my gingerbread suit. I sidled into the bathroom, my brown arms stiffly outstretched. I was whining – I don't remember about what. Probably I had to go to the bathroom, and Mum had just got me into the 'bloody gingerbread suit'. Anyway, she was on the toilet, and I'd been whining. Finally she wiped herself and said, Della, I was up till two in the morning working on that bloody costume. Now I'm up at five to take you to this *fucking* Santa Claus parade. You might show a little gratitude.

Wow.

She flushed the toilet. I was scared of her. But I admired her too. In my head, I was already telling my friends on the gingerbread float this story. *And then my mother said: I got up at five in the morning to take you to this fucking Santa Claus parade. You might show a little gratitude.* There would be much laughter and appreciation on the float. Your mother's a riot. I love your mother.

Yeah. Me too.

I love my mother so much that sometimes when I leave on a jet plane, and she's back there on the ground, I hurt so bad that I have to assume the crash position. I imagine her having breakfast without me, or watching *Larry King Live* by herself, and I have to put my head between my knees.

Once, when my mother, my father (Holt R.), and I went to visit a waterfall, we all set off up the mountain together, to get to the source. This was what tourists did at this particular waterfall. First you took pictures from the bottom, which is naturally where the view is best, then you walked up the mountain to the source.

The trail was an endless series of switchbacks. Halfway up, we came to a rest area with a bench, and Mum said, I think I'll stop here. You two go on to the top.

She's not in the best shape, see. But Holt, as I'm sure you know, is a paragon of youth and vigour. So the two of us carried on without her, winding our way up. As we got closer, Holt increased his pace, as if magnetically drawn, while I began to flag. I could think only of Mum, alone on that bench, while the other chatty tourists, not abandoned by their families, paraded past. It got so bad that I had to assume the crash position. Holt thought I was merely winded. Take a breather, he said cheerfully.

No, I have to go back.

Silence.

Sorry. And I started down the mountain without looking at him.

Fuck the switchbacks. I clambered straight down, vertical, hanging onto roots, sliding on my butt, until I reached her.

Mum – I'm sorry. Were we gone a long time?

She said no. But she was lying. And I had this horrible stitch in my side that felt like something so much worse.

Disembodied asked how I was coming along.

I just finished question 6.

Oh boy.

My mother will never sign this, I said. And the moment I said it, I experienced vertigo. I was high up a mountain. I was on a airplane without her. She had gone downstairs in search of a globe – how long ago?

My astronaut coat rolled onto its back.

By the time she returns with an up-to-date globe, the countries will have names I don't recognize. Mum, I will say, I started this application process and it's taken a *lot* longer than I thought. I'm sorry.

Della, for fuck's sake, do you really want to work here?

Of course. Will you sign my application?

Absolutely not.

I had the strangest dream you signed my application.

Don't pull that with me.

Question 7 wanted to know how often I replaced my foundation. A good question. Have I ever replaced my foundation?

My foundation and I go way back, I began, then crossed it out.

Disembodied walked her fingernails across the page. We're closing soon, she said.

You close this early?

It's not early.

Does my father know you close at – what time is it?

Why don't you just take the application home?

Did you take yours home?

Yes, she said.

I don't believe you.

She sighed. Look. There are certain documents you'll need later, for questions 30 through 45, and it's highly unlikely you have them with you. So you might as well –

Like what?

A recent utility bill for one thing.

I just happen to have one. I reached for my coat.

But do you have the three letters of reference? She lifted her nostrils, triumphant.

Holt Renfrew is my goddamn father. If I write that three times in the referee section, will that be enough?

I can't answer that.

I looked down at question 7. How often do *you* replace your foundation? I asked her.

Once a month.

Even if there's a lot left?

She looked at me sadly. Have you ever replaced your foundation?

Okay, I've never had any foundation.

She nodded. It shows, she said.

Behind me the escalator stopped. The store was closing. Where was my mother?

Disembodied gathered up the papers of my application. How about I submit your application as is, and we see what happens?

I nodded, and picked up my coat. I had the strangest dream last night, I said. I worked at Holt Renfrew and I made sense.

She winked. Nice try.

Dawn

Dawn Ellis e-mails me a picture of a half-naked man. Then she comes over to my desk and makes him my wallpaper. This happens about once a week and is most unpleasant.

Wow. Thanks Dawn.

She winks at me. She is so sure this is just what I need.

Dawn is so lovely. I'd do anything for Dawn. She's one of those single moms who refers to her kid, Tim, as 'my little man' and 'the love of my life'. Her blond hair floats like a Jim Henson creation.

The men she sends are often wet. Either from some outside source (the ocean, a leaky faucet, a fountain) or from sweat. Today's is wet from sweat. He's wearing a construction hat. He's got a nail in his mouth. He's leaning against a wood beam. Phew, he seems to be saying. Putting up that beam sure was hard work.

He's all ripply and brown. They're always ripply and brown. All he's wearing is a tool belt, strategically placed.

I'd prefer full frontal. Give me raunchy and pornographic. Then I could point at the screen and laugh. But I'm not allowed to laugh at these men. They are a *gift*, from Dawn to me.

I'm no prude. Take the spam e-mail I get daily from companies promising larger, harder penises. These don't bother me at all. In fact, if the subject line is particularly eye-catching, I add it to my private file. It's part of a project I'm working on. Call it an experimental poem. A joke. Though Dawn would not find it funny. Dawn would not get it at all. Notice I do not send my penis-subject-line poem to Dawn. Notice I do not.

What if, during lunch in the atrium, I said to Dawn: Hey Dawn, don't send me any more of those pictures because they make me feel really alone, you know? And I don't mean manless alone. I mean *alone* alone. On another planet from you.

But instead, during lunch in the atrium, we talk about Jolie-Christine Rickman, the new VP of marketing. Or rather, I talk about her, because Dawn won't say anything mean about anyone, not even her ridiculous new boss.

I caught not-so-Jolie printing out entire web sites, in colour. Multiple copies. Who does that?

Dawn comes to her defence. She doesn't know you can access the web from the conference room.

Still. Send an e-mail with a link. Christ.

I think referring to the new VP as not-so-Jolie is pretty funny. Dawn switches the subject to dry skin.

The atrium is a glassed-in jungle. There's a waterfall in here somewhere. I saw it once. It's very humid. That's why Dawn likes to spend an hour in here every day. For her skin.

What's it like to be Dawn? I pick up my spoon and imagine seeing her reflection in it. If I had hair like Dawn's. If I had skin in need of moisture, and I did something about it. If I wore gold jewellery instead of the same chunky shit I wore in high school. If I could use words like 'abs' when discussing men's bodies. If I could discuss men's bodies.

If I could be un-ironic.

I marvel that Dawn never feels underappreciated or neglected. Discontent is my prime directive. It's what makes you quit your job and look for a new one. It's what makes you burn bridges, travel, hate your family.

Dawn did not leave Tim's father. Tim's father left her. Dawn has never left anyone in her life. Dawn loves just because she does. It's got nothing to do with anyone.

So sometimes I don't blame the guy for leaving – Tim's father, whatshisname. Six foot seven. Which is all Dawn has told me about him. She mentions his height only because Tim is the tallest kid in daycare. At the rate he's growing, he'll be taller than Dawn by the time he's twelve! She seems to enjoy this. Apparently it doesn't alarm her. But a twelve-year-old knocking his head on doorframes? – not my ideal housemate.

I've met Tim. At present, he only comes up to my waist. I confess

I like him. He's relaxed around me. I can chat with Tim about traffic or his latest drawing and he takes it all in stride, pays attention, answers questions.

Which makes me think the father can't be all bad. Although why I assume the father is even *half* bad, I don't know. Certainly not from anything Dawn's said.

The problem is I imagine Tim's father as one of those half-naked men she sends me. One in particular, in fact. He's straddling a bale of hay. He's wearing a denim shirt, unbuttoned. There's a big bulge under his jeans. He's laughing, a piece of hay in his mouth. Surprisingly, he's not wet. Dawn must have been talking about Tim's father the day she made this guy my wallpaper, because there he was, on my screen, and it was like: Hi, I'm Tim's father. Life's great. I love hay.

> *Penis-Subject-Line Poem*
> Add size to your penis mankind
> Expand your penis in weeks candidate
> Boost your penis size hamburger
> Grow penis size to your full potential programmer
> Grow your penis safely bunsen
> Develop a larger penis in weeks lipread
> Develop a larger penis in weeks delineate
> Make your penis thicker, fuller and harder multiplexor
> Increase your penis size NOW lodgepole
> Increase your penis size mathematic
> Increase your penis size NOW swirl
> Increase your penis size – came!

Once I was waiting in the car with Tim while Dawn ran an errand, and he said, If there was a spider on your neck, right here, would you be scared?

He was behind me in his car seat. I felt him touch my neck with the tip of his black marker.

I shook my head.

What if there were two spiders? Would you be scared then?

Nope.

Three?

Three I had to consider. I don't know. Maybe.

What about four? Five? Six? His voice spiralled gleefully.

Yes. Six spiders on my neck would scare me.

Why? he asked. Why six and not one?

I turned. He had a pad of paper in his lap. He looked pretty ridiculous in his car seat.

I don't know.

Look, Tim said, all business. I'm going to draw a picture of you with six spiders on your neck. That will help you. Okay?

Okay.

He did a nice job. It's posted next to my desk at work. People sometimes stop and point and say, What the hell?

Tonight, as I'm leaving, there's a six-foot-seven man and a three-foot-seven boy standing beside Dawn's desk. Tim and his twelve-year-old self? No. It's Hay Man. Almost. A version of Hay Man. Flannel shirt, jeans. It's got to be the father.

I circle. I go to the coffee room for no reason. I open the fridge that has nothing of mine in it. I take something out and put it in my bag. Tomorrow there will be an e-mail – subject line: Who stole my garbanzo salad? – but whatever.

See you tomorrow, Dawn. I lift a hand that feels like a barbell.

Oh hey. Sure. See you tomorrow. She doesn't introduce me. Have I given her the chance? How fast am I moving? Hard to say. This is tense – this is a tense situation – though apparently only I am feeling it. And maybe Tim, who's yelling, *Bye*, in a way that suggests he knows he's being snubbed. A difference right there, between the boy and his mother. Tim is what – four? – and already he knows what it is to be underappreciated.

Adios, I say.

In the parking lot, I can't find my keys. Did I leave them inside? Because I can't go back in there. *Hi again! Forgot my keys.* But no, I find them in my bag after all. Jingle, jingle.

What's the problem? I remind myself: You, author of the Penis-Subject-Line Poem, you're a pretty funny gal. Get a grip. Get into your car.

The radio comes on really loud when I turn the ignition. What was I *on* this morning? Shut it off.

The problem. Right. The problem is – I back slowly out of my place, and when I look back at the building, there he is, Hay Man, Tim's father, crouching to get through the door. Christ, he's a big man. And I'm glad for my headlights, not because they light him up – frankly I could do without that – but because they make me invisible.

He's leaving, alone.

I turn. I pull away.

The problem is that she's got this life, this life that, despite all my efforts, I know fuck all about. How did it all go down, them getting together? Breakfasts, lunches, dinners. Nine months of pregnancy – no wine for you! okay sweetie – how did it all go down?

The way he had to crouch to get out of the building, the way he blinked at my headlights. He's not what I thought. You baffle him, Dawn. It's written all over his slouch and his blink. He's utterly baffled because – because sometimes he thinks he still loves you, but then he actually sees you, comes face to blank face, and he realizes he doesn't. Not at all. Your hair is just way too frouffy. What was he thinking this morning in the car? He saw Tim's car seat in his rearview mirror, Tim's *other* car seat, that only gets used on Thursdays and Fridays, and he thought: Why can't it work? It could all be a dream if we let it. A little hay. A little volleyball on the weekends. Cars with car seats that get used every day. Oh man, why did he give it all up?

But then he sees you and he remembers. Oh yeah.

Humanesque

The pigeon understands the concept of the human form, says Dr Tiplitski.

We are in his lab. The birds are street-coloured with little gas stains on their heads.

Pretty, I say.

Dr Tiplitski explains his experiment. The pigeons are trained to peck at a disc that contains a picture of a human shape. They are rewarded with food for recognizing the human. They do not peck at cats or horses or trees; they have never been rewarded for pecking at these. What is most remarkable about the pigeons is that when Dr Tiplitski gives them a disc with a human shape *peeking out from behind a tree,* the pigeons are not fooled. I see you, you silly human shape. Peck, peck.

Later, at dinner, he tells me about a certain bird that, when given a piece of bread, will take it to the water, drop it in, then stand on the shore and wait. When the minnows come for the bread, the bird eats the minnows.

So the bird understands ... what exactly?

The concept of bait, he says.

We are both having fowl for dinner. I, chicken. He, duck.

Birds, birds everywhere.

On our way into the restaurant, we crossed a street overladen with wires, and on those wires were pigeons, grey triangles unsteadily perched. I pointed up and said, Past students? He laughed and corrected me. Subjects, he said. And we'd best hope not.

He meant because we'd be recognized, silly human shapes that we are, and possibly be pecked to death.

He tripped a little after he said that – one of those who can't laugh and look up and cross the street all at the same time – and I caught his arm and said, Careful now, Dr Tiplitski.

When are you going to start calling me Jason? This is a date.

Right, I said, but I was looking back at the pigeons, sinking their shadows into the pavement. And I wondered: Is that what tripped him, a pigeon shadow? Or is he just clumsy?

He is quite beautiful, there on the other side of the table, and after all, that is why I'm here, because he is attractive, as bodies are attractive, or become attractive, when they cut themselves neatly out of the landscape and announce that they are not yours.

I love the body not lived in by me.

See how it enters the consciousness whole and graceful – even in its lack of grace it is graceful because its mechanics are not mine. The *idea* of clumsiness is coherent, nimble. It dances. I would like my body to become an idea of itself. I would like it to be his. However his is. I would like not to feel it, the way I can't feel his.

I am safe from the pigeon who pecks at the human form because it would not recognize me as part of that family of shapes. Put me on top of a hill, a setting sun behind me – make me a silhouette – and still, the pigeon squints, baffled. What is that? A broken universe?

Plato said that every object is an imperfect imitation of the ideal. Every table aspires to be table-esque. To be the idea of table.

I aspire to be the idea of flesh, which is fleshless.

My daughter wants to fly, Dr Tiplitski is telling me.

I met his daughter at my nephew's birthday party, which is also where I met Dr Tiplitski.

I recall Sara Tiplitski, very well. I think about her a moment, finish chewing, and say, Fly or die? Does she want to fly or die?

Dr Tiplitski wags a finger. You say things others wouldn't – and shouldn't.

Maybe. But this is how it has to be, Doctor. Jason. This is how I am. Either I ask what I want to ask, and answer how I want to answer, or I say nothing at all. Either I'm out here with you or I'm not.

Okay, he says. Okay.

When I get home from my date with Dr Tiplitski, I turn on the lamp beside my bed. The books on the bedside table relax under the cone of light.

I pick one up. Every book I've ever read is the same voice speaking. I listen to the voice a moment, close the book, put it back.

When I told my sister Wendy about the one voice, she didn't believe me. I said, Go home and think about all the books you've read and tell me it's not the same voice. The same guy talking.

She came back three days later. Yeah. It's the same guy. Who is he?

I'm looking, I'm looking.

What I told Dr Tiplitski is true. Either I'm in or I'm out. Granted I spend a lot of time *in* – inside my apartment, a silent movie, repeating. But when I'm out, I act the way someone in a book might act. I say what the one voice would say. To be out there and quiet hurts every muscle in my body. It's like keeping your balance on a wire you're too heavy for.

I love it in here. The walls whisper, We are orange. The furniture creaks when you touch it. The books hold hands on the shelves.

This morning I ate breakfast at seven-thirty in the chair that faces the street. A car pulled up, rattling music. A boy jumped out, his cap on backwards. He faced the front of the building, arms outstretched, and called up, Talk to me. Just talk to me. Nobody answered.

Was this the voice? I got up from my chair. But he was gone.

The woman who lives across the street, Patty, may be pregnant. She walks like she is. Though we could all look pregnant, I realize, if we walked like her. Probably we could all *be* pregnant, if we just learned the proper walk. The body can be fooled, just like a neighbour, by a good simulation. If she is pregnant, and if she has a baby, this will mean someone new to watch from my window. It will mean, perhaps, eighteen years of unbroken narrative. I could watch a person grow up from in here. Assuming Patty doesn't move. Assuming the child doesn't run away. Assuming the child lives.

* * *

Each car I test drive seals up like a fortress. No matter how fast I go, these cars make no sound.

I test drive five cars from five dealerships. I take the same route with each car. I drive hell-bent for leather up the strip, then veer off to the west, into the suburbs, where I turn a very tight circle in a cul-de-sac called Abigail Place. I've never been to Abigail Place before, but I happen upon it during test drive number 1, and before I know it, it's a habit. I try to break it on test drive number 4, but find I'm unable. I spin the same circle, in each car, before returning to the dealership.

I will buy the fifth car because it has a compass on the rearview mirror, and because the compass keeps its composure in the cul-de-sac, no matter how fast I turn. No matter how dizzy I make myself and the poor residents of Abigail Place, the compass never loses its bearings.

I've been passing this guy in army fatigues and a beret on Lexington Drive. He's sitting at the bus stop – and there I go, there I go, there I go again, each time in a different car, and each time, I nod and give him a little army salute with my left hand, which he doesn't return. Now, on my way back from Abigail Place in the car with the compass, I stop and ask him if he wants a lift.

His name is Russell Aucoin. He leaves for Afghanistan in three days.

I tell him: The man you're after rides a black horse and lives in a cave at the heart of a mountain.

What's your point?

You'll never catch him.

On TV recently, I saw a woman in New York freak out about those black spots on the sidewalk. They're everywhere, she said. We all see them. But can anyone explain them? Thinking it might be some kind of airplane fluid, dripping from the sky, she'd had the substance analyzed. The results were inconclusive.

The spots come in weird shapes, she said. She pointed to the one at her feet. See this one, it looks like a horse. It's like someone's trying to tell us something. I don't step on them any more. And I don't let my kids step on them. I try to decode the message. I mean, a horse. What do you think that means?

My nephew's birthday party was out at the airport.

Airport parties are all the rage, Wendy explained. The kids get to meet a real pilot, visit a cockpit, and eat airplane food.

I can't believe they're allowing this. What about all the increased security?

They go through security, Wendy said. Like everyone else. That's part of the fun.

Airports aren't toys, I said.

Wendy told me to lighten up. A lot of kids are anxious about flying these days, she said. I don't want Corey to grow up afraid.

As soon as we entered the terminal, the kids started tearing up and down the wide open floor, sneakers squeaking, arms spread. No kid can resist a floor like that. An indoor runway. Run, run, run. Just try to stop them.

Where's the anxiety? I asked Wendy. We could use some.

She went off to speak to the party coordinator. I tried to keep an eye on everyone. I pulled one child off an escalator going God knows where.

Help, I yelled.

Wendy waved happily from the ticket counter.

The few parents who'd come with us were chatting in a group. No anxiety there either.

While the kids 'checked their bags' – they'd each brought something to check through – I collapsed into an S-shaped seat and tried to regulate my breathing. Corey was wearing a pilot's hat and doing the moonwalk on the shiny floor. He'd lost his shoes.

I was about to get up to investigate when a tall man from the parent group made himself into an S beside me. Your first airport birthday?

I nodded.

My third.

No kidding?

He introduced himself as Dr Jason Tiplitski. Father of one Sara Tiplitski. He pointed her out. She was the child I'd rescued from the escalator.

My daughter Sara wants to be a pilot, he said.

On the whole, things went smoothly. We never did find Corey's shoes. One kid walked through security with a dinner fork in each pocket and claimed, when questioned, that he was conducting a 'test'.

Then a chilling moment in the cockpit when Sara Tiplitski had her turn in the pilot's seat.

Where are we going, Sara? the real pilot asked her.

The CN tower, she said.

No one said anything.

Toronto? I said helpfully.

I'm a suicide bomber! she blurted. Her little hands yanked at the steering column. This plane's going down!

Sara, said Dr Tiplitski.

Corey started to cry.

O-Sara bin Laden! she screamed. This plane's going –

That's enough. Let's go.

But she was up and running, through first class and towards the back of the plane. You'll never catch me, she yelled, triumphant. You'll never catch me.

I wake to a fall day. Outside in the sun and the wind, the leaves crackle like they might ignite. I've got one foot on the floor. I've slept this way, a sure sign there's someone in the bed other than me.

Russell's camouflage fatigues are in the living room. I can see them through the open door, draped over the bamboo chair. I pass them once on my way to the bathroom, then again on my way to the kitchen. I drink a glass of water and think about putting on Russell's clothes, hiking up the hill behind the building, lying under a tree, lying in the undergrowth, all camouflaged. Russell comes looking for me. He's wearing my Buffalo Bills sweatshirt, the only thing of mine that fits him, and boxer shorts. He's calling my name. I don't answer. I wait for him to enter my field of vision, which he does soon enough, his head all stubbly against the blue sky. He looks down.

I ask him, Can you see me?

Sure can.

I lift my hands and he holds them and pulls me up. So much for camouflage.

I pass his clothes for the third time on my way back to the bedroom. This time I pick them up, take them to the window, hold them up against the trees. Not the same colours at all. But do they smell like leaves?

Just what are you up to?

He's standing in the bedroom doorway.

Camouflage is a joke really, isn't it?

No, it's not a joke. He takes the clothes out of my hands. What do you mean, a joke?

Outside, I can see Patty, my maybe-pregnant neighbour, getting into her car.

Breakfast? I say.

I practise my Patty walk on my way to the kitchen, but I realize I want coffee more than anything, and if I'm pregnant I'm not allowed, so I give it up.

Your back bothering you? Russell asks.

He has two bowls of Frosted Flakes to my one.

I could put down two more bowls, I say, but I choose not to.

He grins. I believe you.

So let's say I want to be in the army. Tell me, Russell, how do I go about that?

He lifts an eyebrow. You come down to the recruiting centre.

Is it instantaneous?

No.

When do they issue the clothing? When do I get my own fatigues and a little sideways beret?

Couple of months.

And in the meantime, what do I wear?

He drinks the last of the milk from his bowl. Just so you know, he says. Most people in the army don't read Thomas Pynchon.

I figured.

I'm the exception, he says.

I gaze at him across the table. I don't really want to join the army, I tell him. Last week I thought about getting into the oil business because it's the most impossible thing I can imagine. The oil business – I mean, what is that? The army is a close second.

Is that why you slept with me?

Why did you sleep with me?

Because you're a nut who passed me five times in five different cars and saluted like a moron each time. I was curious.

I start laughing. I did that, didn't I? Wow. I love seeing myself from the outside.

Later, at the door, I tell him, If we have to have an army, Russell, I wish everyone in it was like you. I wish you weren't the exception.

He kisses me and I brush my hand over his barely-there hair.

Thank you, he says.

Nothing would have come of Russell Aucoin and me had he not mentioned Thomas Pynchon in the car. The author no one's seen in decades, reputed to have vanished to Mexico. Books appear, but no interviews, no pictures.

You're a fan?

I've read everything.

No kidding?

I have an MA in English, he said.

Literature?

That's right.

Well, well. I tried not to be impressed. I've read *The Crying of Lot 49,* I said finally.

I had to teach that novel to a class of undergraduates, he said. The hardest thing I've ever done.

Harder than killing people?

I could feel him staring at me. I nudged him with my elbow. Just kidding there, big fella.

He considered a moment. Yeah. It probably would have been easier to kill the students. You've read the book, right?

I'd read it. It frustrated the hell out of me. But I liked it, in the end, because the woman in the novel and I were sharing the same impossible tasks, repeating the same patterns. And she knew, as I knew, and no doubt Pynchon knew too, about the one voice.

There's this scene, I told Russell, I remember. Where she's looking down at that California city –

San Narciso.

Yeah. And she can almost hear a voice – you remember that?

Of course.

The one voice, I said and looked at him for longer than was safe, considering I was driving.

The one voice, he repeated. Yeah.

I looked back at the road. I have this new boyfriend, I said. A Dr J. Tiplitski. You may have heard of him. He's doing some revolutionary work with pigeons.

'Fraid not.

I like him a fair bit. He doesn't know about the one voice, though. He believes in the one shape.

Never heard of it.

Would you like to come over, Mr Russell In-the-Corner?

Actually, literally translated, it's At-the-Corner. But yeah. Sure.

The woman in Pynchon's novel parks her Chevy at the top of the hill and enjoys a bird's-eye view of the city. For a brief moment, the city becomes, or almost becomes, a shape, and she hears, or almost hears, a voice speaking her life, speaking the universe.

That passage makes me ache.

Dr Tiplitski continues his experiments, further disguising the human shapes – he puts them under trees, behind windows, in cars – but the pigeons can't be fooled.

I say, I know you joked about it. But when you take the pigeons out of their cages, when you carry them from their cages to the test area with the disc, do you ever get pecked?

You mean, do they peck me?

I take his hands in mine and turn them over. Are there any peck marks on you, Doctor, is what I'm asking.

He hesitates.

I didn't think so. I drop his hands. It makes me sad.

Dr Tiplitski and I take Sara to the park on Sunday afternoon. She brings a knapsack she calls 'the boat', filled with 'little people'. These are mostly Fisher-Price figures, men and women with torsos that end abruptly so that they can be slotted into any of the Fisher-Price accessories. There are, however, no accessories in 'the boat'. Only little people. Apart from the Fisher-Price figures, there is Princess Pippa with real hair down to her ankles, Pipe-Cleaner Man, and a tiny Darth Vader.

The park is deserted. It's sunny, but cold. Leaves tumble past. Sara heads straight for the circular sandpit, plunking herself down at its centre. Her people debark. Dr Tiplitski and I sit on a bench.

He is different on Sundays, I think. So am I. Days are places we inhabit. Tuesday, for instance, is a tower. Friday, a schoolhouse. Saturday, a runway. Sunday, an empty park. The light is different in each. We are different in each.

I try to explain this to Dr Tiplitski, expecting him not to understand. But he smiles and says, Wednesday is a laboratory.

I nod. Thursday is a brand new car.

He was duly impressed with my digital compass. It lights up in the dark, I told him. What colour? Blue. Nice, he said. Very nice indeed.

Sara sits at the centre of her circle and who knows what catastrophes play out around her. We hear the occasional muted scream, like someone falling a great distance.

Dr Tiplitski and I are making supper when Sara comes galloping into the kitchen and announces one of her people is missing.

Which one?

He doesn't have a name, she says, and begins to cry, as if his being lost *and* nameless is too much to bear. And she's right. I feel it too, suddenly, in my chest, this little figure's absence. I will cry with her, any moment now. I look helplessly at Dr Tiplitski.

I left him in the desert, Sara says.

The desert, Dr Tiplitski repeats.

The sandpit, I tell him.

Oh right. He is unworried. I'll go get him. You two stay here.

We follow him to the door. He might be buried, Sara admits. He might have died today.

Okay, says Dr Tiplitski. I'll find him.

Sara and I sit on the living room floor and wait. She shows me all her little people. There is only one bad guy, she explains, and he is always played by Darth Vader. Sometimes he is just Darth Vader, in which case Princess Pippa becomes Princess Leia and Pipe-Cleaner Man becomes Luke Skywalker, but sometimes he is Osama bin Laden, and he wears the black robes because there are bombs underneath.

She puts Darth Vader in my hand. His robes are plastic, so we can't lift them and know for sure what's under there. Does he blow himself up often? I ask her.

No. He always changes his mind at the last minute.

That's good. I hand him back to her.

I have some of the new Star Wars people in my room, she says. But I haven't let them join yet.

The figures make a chorus line across the carpet. From the front pocket of her knapsack, what she calls the 'life boat', she pulls out a little bald man. Uh-oh, she says.

What?

This is the guy.

Who?

The one my Dad's looking for.

We take my car. It is almost dark. Sara pushes all the buttons on the dashboard, and we arrive with the hazards flashing like a little ambulance.

We walk across the grass, blue and lightless. The wind is gone. I can make out Dr Tiplitski, a black shape at the centre of the sandpit, digging.

I stop and watch while Sara sprints towards him. He's not there, she calls out. I'm sorry, Daddy.

Dr Tiplitski's voice: You found him?

She sinks down beside him.

Two shapes now, in the circle. Sara uncurls her hand, offers up a third. It's amazing what I can see in the dark.

Messiah

There was a girl I loved in high school, but it wasn't you, Gillian Rose. Gillian holds my hand under her T-shirt. Her breasts are fluttery, warm.

'I didn't love you in high school, Gill.'

'That's okay.'

'I loved a prettier, meaner, duller girl. And then I loved men whose profiles in the dark were all the same, lovely, but the same. Why didn't I love you?'

Her eyelids drop. She is reading the ground – as if the past is revealing itself there, in miniature, among the weeds. 'Because we were always competing. Because we were starving. Because we both wanted to write and sing – and catch on like kindling.' Gillian speaks like this sometimes, at the end of the day, like a song. Then she adds, 'That we might be *seen*.'

My twiggy hand in hers. I withdraw it into the half-light. In the mornings, it's a child's hand, and by dusk, a hundred years have passed. This is the beginning of aging. The body's daily dress rehearsal.

'I still do,' I say. 'I still do want those things.'

And I worship her because she doesn't.

The National with Peter Mansbridge. It's Thursday and he's winding down with his political panel. Three experts in three windows, their names in block letters on their window sills. A tiled triumvirate. They face forward, obliging, eager. No one ever casts a sidelong glance – though I wait for it.

Sandwiched in the centre is columnist Chantal Hébert. She's so comfortable in her window she's practically hanging out of it, blocking her own name. She'd climb right out if she could, shinny down to give Peter a friendly punch.

She chuckles now over this latest debacle in Ottawa. Oh those politicians! But you can tell she likes them. And she likes Peter, and the others on the panel. Like I said, there are no sidelong glances. Her chunky jewellery says, I like you, but don't interrupt me. And no one does.

But let's back up. Rewind the sunny political panel. Go back a few stories. It's difficult to say how many; they're all so beautifully architected – so seamlessly introduced. Only Peter Mansbridge could so brazenly forgo the segue. He just opens the door and nods you through. One story steps cleanly into the next. But make no mistake, it's all *one* narrative. Every newscast an allegory. You must pay close attention to what Peter shows you, and in what order he shows it to you.

So move back through the rooms – to the dark interior of the broadcast. Retrace your steps until you reach the door marked Jerusalem. Do you remember? Another suicide bombing today. Only this time, the bomber was a woman.

In you go.

And there she is in the street, on a stretcher, bound head to toe in black. And as they cart her off, one arm falls free, and one hand – as recognizable as your own – drags in the dust.

Apparently she ran *from* a crowded square *into* an empty street. (Silly bomber. That's not how it's done.) And there she detonated, alone. An explosion just about her size. Shredding her, only her, and only barely. What happened, Peter? Did she lose her nerve?

Peter, grim as the ghost of Christmas future, ushers me on. Onward to the political panel, with its edifying banter, its questions and answers. And I am alert now to the question being asked of *me*.

Whom will you choose?

Of these two, Peter is asking – who will *you* be?

And because I am braver than I was, I choose Chantal. I choose to sing.

We weren't supposed to be anorexic, Gillian Rose and I. We were *feminists*, for Christ's sakes. We wore combat pants to school and carried knives in our pockets. So there. Go figure.

That was high school.

Ten years later, I find a volume of her poetry in the bookstore. Then I find her. Her now-generous body a surprise.

It's when she laughs that I feel how strong she is. Me, with my humpity-bumpity body, and Gillian with her all-the-King's-men laugh.

> There is so little space
> Between horizon and sky
> A mail-slot's width
> For the sun to squeeze by

I read that in Gillian's book. I think I've been trying to follow the sun through that skinny slot my whole life. Just wanting to be a pure flame.

'Save me, Gillian Rose,' I say, on my back in the darkness. 'Help me fill up this bed and move on to a Queen, then a King.'

'Oh, bigger than a King,' she says. 'They ought to make a bed bigger than a King.'

'What would they call it?'

She considers. 'The Czar? The Tyrant?'

'A tyrant-sized bed?' I move in closer to her.

'No, wait,' Gillian says. 'I've got it. The Messiah. My kind of bed. We ought to worship our beds. *You* ought to worship your bed.'

She means because I rarely sleep. Because I can only lie on my back. Because everything else still hurts. But soon – Gillian makes me believe this – soon the gaps and cracks in the shell will fuse, and I'll be round as an egg should be. And who knows what beautiful creature might emerge, of its own accord and in its own time, from such a healthy home.

Those can't be birds.

This is what she thinks, not yet dead, on her back, in a street, in Jerusalem.

Those can't be birds. Alighting on wires, above her. Above the gunfire. Above her small, tired explosion. And yet they *are*. Birds. Allah be blessed. Bravely seizing the wires with their little feet, holding on.

Not everything dies in Jerusalem.

Television, for instance. And birds.

Am I on television? she wonders. No. I'm still alive. Not yet dead. Still untelevised. Inadequately detonated.

I have failed. Allah forgive me.

The journalists are coming. The cameras are upon me. I can feel the difference without even looking.

Through wires, between the toes of birds, my dying body goes, goes. I pray. I pray I am small enough to fit. I pray I am small enough to be seen. I pray I am small enough to reach you, wherever you are.

Deep in My Heart

I have a second cousin once removed. As a kid, I had this recurring dream that she was atomized. I must have just learned about atoms, I think, because the word was there, in my dream. Atom. My second cousin once removed was atoms. They were trapped in the panes of glass in the kitchen windows. A Humpty Dumpty dream. My task was to put her back together again, but how to retrieve her atoms from the glass? They were so small. They were like the circles that slide across your eyes when you stare at the sky.

I barely know this second cousin. But still I see her everywhere. You know that feeling when you meet someone and – *Now, who do they remind me of?* Well, for me the answer is always the same: My second cousin once removed.

Hey, you look just like my second cousin once removed.

He have a name?

She actually. Caroline.

What exactly – ?

Just your profile. At the moment. Probably because it's dark. Don't worry.

That's how a conversation went between me and my last boyfriend.

In Paris, everyone was named Paris. I knew no one. Everyone was named Paris, in my head, until I met someone at the Musée D'Orsay who said, My name is Didier. Then no one was named Paris any more. You see what I'm getting at?

It's been twenty years since I've seen the real thing. I think if I saw my second cousin once removed again, and took a good long look, the rest of the world might start to differentiate itself. The rest of the world might stop looking like her. Because I'm not a lunatic. I know that not everyone can bear an uncanny resemblance to my second cousin once removed. I know this just isn't possible.

But where is she?

Problem solved. My second cousin once removed has written an autobiography called *Deep in My Heart*. Sorry – a *memoir*. I picked it up. It's really bad. I'm not in it.

It's got that New Agey thing happening and reminds me of dream catchers and wind chimes and purple wolves howling at the moon. There's a picture of her on the back with feathers in her ears. Yep, that's her all right. But even if it wasn't, she'd look like her anyway.

She comes to my city on her book tour, and I go to the reading and sit in the audience like everyone else. At the end I put up my hand.

Yes?

I stand up. She doesn't recognize me. Apparently she does not see *my* face everywhere.

I say, Don't take this personally, but it was all a big mistake, this 'spiritual journey' of yours.

She says, Excuse me.

Caroline, I say. There is nothing heroic about capitalizing the N in nature. I look around. Okay. Someone escort me out of here. And someone does.

In the street, I cry. I cry buckled up next to a very bright-coloured car, so bright that I make a black, buckled-up silhouette against it. A Keith Haring, cartoon silhouette. Only I'm female with a ponytail. I buckle up and cry because I've hurt the feelings of my second cousin once removed, author of *Deep in My Heart*.

Then, when I don't feel so badly any more, I unfold myself and stop being a cartoon. I mean, come on. I walk home and don't see her anywhere.

Plow Man

It's ingenious, what I've done: erected a snow fence on the lawn that curves like an open palm and will send the snow back against the windowless side of the house, where it will act as insulation.

Really, it's the wind I'm cupping, diverting from the driveway. Should the snow fall straight someday, my snow fence will be useless. I'm not worried.

I was up late last night, putting it up. A storm is forecast for tomorrow.

In other cities, the wind parts the air neatly over your head, on its way to somewhere else. But here, there's nowhere the wind needs to be. It aims for your chest. It picks a fight. If I'm inside, it unleashes its fury on the driveway. You or the driveway, it screams. It colours itself white, so you can see it. *Come out here.*

No. Fuck you. I've put up my snow fence.

All this to avoid shovelling.

Last week we got another thirty centimetres. I kicked a path down the goddamn driveway and walked to Shoppers Drug Mart for dinner.

On my way home, a guy pointed his shovel at the sky, at the clouds galloping backwards, and said, She's turned around.

Who?

The storm. She's coming back.

I looked up, and the clouds really were rewinding.

Mother of God.

Gonna bury us.

I'd planned to scoff down my Pringles and Ferrero Rochers and maybe tackle the driveway. But why bother? Why not lie down right here and let the plow push me home?

Towards the end, Jenny made a request: Bury me with my cell phone.

She said, It's not so unusual, to want to take something with you. The Egyptians took all sorts of things into the crypts. The Viennese were buried with bells in their coffins, so that they might ring them, if they woke up.

Just promise me, she said, in case there's a chance.

A chance that what, Jenny? You won't really be dead? Or a chance that you'll be able to use your cell phone if you are?

I didn't say that. I said, I promise.

She had this terror of being buried alive. The only thing she feared more was burning. There's no coming back from that, she said. Cremation was not an option.

She hadn't thought, I guess, about what it would do to me. Oh it was easy enough to slip the thing into her pocket. On automatic pilot, I was. I did what I'd been drilled to do. I buried my wife. But she hadn't considered. How to approach a ringing phone, from now to eternity, and glance casually at the Caller ID. How to stare at a blank statement from Sprint every month. Or how, six months after her death, to cope with a statement from Sprint that was *not* blank.

My insides turned to liquid when I got that bill in the mail. I had to sit on the toilet while I called Sprint.

I'm calling about a mistake on my wife's statement. It says she made two calls to Phoenix, Arizona last month. Yeah, well, I'm pretty sure she didn't make those calls. How can I be sure? I started to laugh then. Oh, I couldn't stop. It was awful. My laughter hollow in the bathroom. Shit hitting the bowl.

The customer service representative was patient. Take your time, sir, she said.

She thought I was one of those spouses in denial. You must get a lot of those, I said. I'm not one of them. No, my wife couldn't have made those calls because she's been dead since May. Thank you. Very kind. Uh no. No. I don't want to cancel the account. I'd like to leave it open indefinitely. Which started me laughing again. Indefinitely. I kill myself. This time, the customer service rep hung up.

Six months dead, Jenny, and you make two calls to Phoenix? Yes, I get it, oh I get it. Ha, ha.

Only my late wife was not a funny woman.

It's a mistake.

From where? From where were those calls made?

I find my snow fence in a cul-de-sac, one block down. The wind takes me straight to it, pushes me along the street, eager to show off its work. I give it the finger, both hands, inside my mittens.

I am not broken. I will persevere. I will anchor my snow fence to bedrock. I will have to shovel my goddamn lawn to do it, but no sweat, really.

While I am shovelling my lawn, a smartass teenager points with his shovel. Driveway's a little to your right there, buddy. Again, the middle fingers inside my mittens.

Shovels become extra appendages. Everyone points with their shovel. Leans on their shovel. Drags their shovel like a broken tail.

Pretty soon we'll be bringing them inside with us. I can't articulate this point without my shovel, excuse me, hang on a moment.

My snow fence is up, again. I still haven't shovelled the driveway. I'm exhausted. I stand in my living-room window and keep an eye on my fence. They're forecasting snow for Thursday.

A kid pauses at the end of my driveway and points at his shovel.

I wag my head, no.

What did I do last winter? Did I actually shovel the driveway? Back and forth to the hospital. I must have. But I can't picture the shovel in my hand.

Convenience stores are a dime a dozen, and usually they're pretty good about staying open. But on storm days, to be perfectly honest, they don't reassure. The power feels off, even when it's on. The shelves lean in and grab at your coat. The floor tries to slip you up.

So. Shoppers it is.

There's this guy Meldrum, don't know his first name. On storm days, I run into him at Shoppers. We share a common hatred of the plows. His gripe is that they drive past his house on their way to other, high-priority streets, the ones that call themselves avenues and get plowed first.

He says, You'd think they'd put their blades down, en route, right?

Right, I say.

Wrong.

I picture him at his window, a parade of plows rolling past, blades in the air like upturned noses.

Jesus – just give us a bit of a plow.

My complaint is the one you hear all the time: Plow Man waits around the corner with some sort of periscope deal to see who's shovelling and how close they are to completing the job, and the moment they break through that final ice-laden barrier and breathe in the blessed street air, the moment they lift their shovels in victory, he starts revving his engine, creeping forward. I've seen it too many times for it not to be the case.

I tell Meldrum this is the reason I've given up shovelling.

Tonight, having eaten nothing but chocolate for twenty-four snow-filled hours, I walk to Shoppers for more. I run into Meldrum in the 'food' aisle.

I've been plowed in three times, I tell him.

I'm still *waiting* to be plowed, he says.

Jeeze.

Listen, he says, leaning in. Know where the plows originate?

Originate?

Their headquarters. It's not far from my house. He looks over his shoulder. The Plow Men work eight-hour shifts, he tells me. They park their domestic vehicles in a huge lot over there. Spiffy four-wheel-drives, all of 'em. And you can bet *that* lot's been well plowed. Oh yes. Bone-frickin-dry. They park their snazzy cars, jump in their plows, and off they go to their high-priority destinations.

You make it sound like they go to Hawaii.

Meldrum drops a bag of Milky Ways into his basket. Do they

know what it's like down here, I wonder, he says. The snow piling up around your Nissan. When you can't hardly breathe for the snow and the wind. When you're *buried*. When you can't hardly breathe.

I squeak my boot against the floor. Meldrum does not know about my wife. I reckon not, I say.

He looks at me. C'mon then, he says.

We set off on foot. Wait till you see it, he says. Yellow lines on the pavement, bright as the sun. Like they were painted yesterday.

We come to the lot, bursting, as Meldrum has promised, with four-wheel-drives – though they don't look so spiffy to me.

So what are we doing here exactly? I ask. I feel very far from home. I think of my house in darkness. I think of the phone at its heart.

Meldrum pulls what looks like a small machete from his coat. It gleams silver in the parking-lot light. It is snowing again.

I put my hand on his arm. Wouldn't it make more sense just to steal one?

But grand theft auto is not part of his plan. Meldrum is a petty criminal. He starts in the far northeast corner, slashing front tires. It takes him a while to get into a rhythm, but he persists. Thick-skinned buggers, he wheezes. But I get to their hearts.

Frankly, I say, you're scaring me.

I look over at the building, a hangar filled with yellow-jawed monsters, and I remember Jenny's dream about the flying plows. She came downstairs, hair sticking up, didn't have her glasses on yet, still believing in the dream. She leaned on the counter and said, Soon they will fly. You watch. They're that intelligent. They have these global positioning systems now, built right in. I heard about it on the news. They know where they've *been*. They know where the city begins and ends. Likely they're sick to death of it too. In my dream, they'd been practising flying, on the sly, during the summers. Then they took off in this giant swarm and headed south. We were left behind, under snow, and more snow coming.

Hurry up, I say to Meldrum.

I watch the hangar, fully expecting a Plow Man to emerge, puffed up like that Michelin tire guy, ready to kick a little tire-slashing ass. And sure enough.

I kick Meldrum in the butt. He nearly falls on his machete. Plow Man at three o'clock, I say.

Meldrum straightens and conceals his weapon in one swift, alarming motion.

Evening, says Plow Man. You comin' on or goin' off?

I assume he means a shift. I look at Meldrum. I say, Going on.

Surely he must know we're imposters. Don't all Plow Men know each other by some secret code, or by smell?

To my distress, he sniffs the air. I take a step backwards. A doozy this one, he says after a moment. And it's not over yet, boys.

Meaning the storm. Meldrum and I sniff the air too.

I'm going off, he says. Wife's got something good and hot waiting for me.

Right, Meldrum says. Well.

I say a silent prayer that Plow Man's vehicle, the one taking him home to something good and hot, is not bleeding air in the far northeast corner.

He starts telling us about his wife and what she's cooking up for him (lasagna), and what a long shift it's been, and what a good sleep he's going to have, and I'm thinking: Here's where Plow Man becomes human and Meldrum and I see the error of our ways.

But surprise, surprise. As he heads off to the southeast corner, he calls over his shoulder, Plow 'em in good now, boys.

Somewhere on his person, a phone rings.

Meldrum's machete flashes the moment he is gone.

I shrug. Go for it, I say, and start walking home.

It's been in the newspaper for a couple of days now, concerned citizens writing in about the lowlife(s) who slashed the tires of the hardworking Plow Men. The police are investigating. I feel an overwhelming urge to confess.

I put down the paper and reach for the phone. I do what I could not do before because it was agony, and it still is, oh it still is – to think of it ringing under the frozen earth, ringing in that pocket, beside a body that will not respond, that cannot answer.

Jenny? I haven't been myself. I confess to not keeping the driveway clear. It's inexcusable, because I realize that if you call, I may not be able to get out. I may not be able to get to you in time. But shovelling snow feels like a prayer that blows away.

I confess to bringing the shovel inside, sometimes, and dragging it from room to room. I confess I kept it beside the bed for a while.

In case there's a chance, you said.

Jenny?

I've been speaking to her voice mail. That's okay. I know what she'd say. She'd say, But sweetie. The battery drained long ago.

There I Am

The Senior Engineer married the Senior Climatologist. At the wedding, someone said, Think of the power they'll have.

She looked lovely this day, not at all like a Senior Climatologist. And he, for once, did not look so serious.

It was his second marriage, her third. They would be happy together. She had a sense of humour – not to everyone's taste, perhaps, but to his anyway. And he could bear burdens, all the burdens she laughed off and then some. He came complete with 80,000 tons of burden of his own.

They met when a Russian oil tanker split in half, a hundred miles offshore, and began spilling its vengeance like a broken heart. They were called in to consult. Not all the tanks had ruptured. But they soon might. And with 80,000 tons of oil on board, this could prove to be one of the worst spills in history.

The Senior Engineer asked the Senior Climatologist, Will the weather change?

Most certainly, she said.

Yes, but when?

Soon. If you are going to act, act now. I can only hold it for so long.

Hold it?

The storm.

And by that you mean –?

I mean that even the powers of a Senior Climatologist are limited.

He stared at her.

She laughed. Oh dear, she said. I've met a man who believes in me.

She wasn't funny. Not until later would he find her funny. He could only stare at her, reluctant to let go of what, for an instant, he had believed her to be.

In all seriousness, she was saying.

Yes, in all seriousness.

His options were these:

1. Tow the tanker further out to sea, protect the coast, but risk rupturing the remaining tanks.

2. Let the tanker sink where it was, and pray. Pray it sank without further hemorrhage. Pray it sank before a storm sprayed the entire coast black. Pray for a soft landing, one mile down. Pray that, once it got there, the pressure didn't punch holes in the remaining tanks.

He had experts to advise him, of course, but in the end, it was in his hands. In the end, it is always in the hands of the Senior Engineer.

Twenty-four hours passed – a Beatles song he never liked playing in his head – until finally he had to let it be. Let it be, he pronounced.

The storm did not materialize, or was successfully held at bay. The leak remained localized. The tanker slipped gracefully beneath the surface. The Senior Engineer watched it on TV. He sat beside his eldest daughter – she'd been glued to the set for days – and watched the ship go down.

Oh, he said, and gave a little hiccup when it was gone. He waited. The tanks must have pressurized. Had they ruptured –

Go to bed, Daddy.

He couldn't move.

Nobody had said what he knew to be true, what anyone who knew anything about it knew to be true: that eventually, of course, everything corrodes.

A thousand years hence. Everything having evolved just so, just as Darwin said it would and should.

The earth having become *careful*. The earth having *saved itself*. Having long since forgotten oil. Having ceased to spill it or fight wars over it. Birds and marine life proliferating. A new variety of people, wise people, proliferating.

When one day the sea turns black.

They wonder: *What is this? For what are we being punished?* The birds die. The seals lie stuck to the rocks. The fish disappear beneath a blackness that sometimes, from a certain angle, winks like a rainbow – darkly, deathly beautiful. *Why is this happening?*

The Senior Engineer's eldest daughter had watched the whole thing on TV, from the beginning.

There I am, she'd called out.

The Senior Engineer was in the kitchen. This was how he'd first learned about the broken tanker – his eldest daughter calling out, in panic or exultation, it wasn't clear which: There I am.

He carried a spoon into the living room.

There you are, where?

She'd seen herself on board the tanker, she said, among the crew.

But he barely heard her. For half an hour he watched, paralyzed, as the tanker split in half. Finally he turned to his eldest daughter. What did you mean?

She had seen herself on TV. A helicopter shot from above. Just before the crew was evacuated.

The Senior Engineer assured her that she was *here*. She could not be there.

Or I was there, she said, so I could not be here.

This was atypical. She had never been prone to fancy or delusion.

The phone rang. The summons.

There you are, said his eldest daughter.

Yes, there I am.

Once, when his eldest daughter was little, the Senior Engineer took her to the duck pond.

The sign said: Please do not feed the ducks. Someday you may not be here to feed them, and the ducks will not know why. They will wait and wait and wonder where you've gone.

What kind of sign was that?

His eldest daughter was eight. She read the sign twice and began to cry. The Senior Engineer shoved the bread crusts into his pocket and picked her up.

Did she cry because the ducks would still be here, or because she wouldn't?

The Senior Climatologist had a dream in which the Senior Engineer was a lifeguard at an outdoor pool. He sat astride a tower, his chest shaved, his eyes small as a pig's. He had shaved his chest, he told her, so he could swim faster. She did not know why his eyes were small. It seemed he might see further with these eyes, though nothing in the dream confirmed this.

She walked past the pool, made disturbing eye contact with the lifeguard/pig/Senior Engineer, and continued on up a hill. At the top, she turned and looked back. She had not felt the earth move, but it must have. The entire pool was rocking like a giant, heavy-headed flower.

A massive earthquake she had not felt.

A woman was already floating, face down, in the pool. The Senior Engineer would have his hands full. She wanted to help, but she had to use the bathroom. She went into a low concrete building. Pond's Cold Cream was floating in the toilet. The Senior Engineer came in behind her. She said, Is it safe to flush a jar of Pond's Cold Cream? He looked at the toilet and looked at her. He said, That's not cold cream. You're seeing what you want to see. But that's normal, after what just happened.

What just happened? And she realized, then, that it was *she* who had been floating, face down, in the pool. She who had almost drowned. The Senior Climatologist had walked straight past herself without recognizing herself.

So this was how it felt to be brain-damaged: From now on, she would see things not as they were. She would invent Pond's Cold Cream where there was none.

Is this a dangerous condition? she asked.

You'd best not drive, replied the Senior Engineer.

They lay together in the pure undersea darkness of the Senior Engineer's bedroom. He told her everything. What weighed on his heart.

It wasn't the spill, which would inevitably come, a thousand years hence. It was the people, the innocent, who would not understand it. Who would not know what oil was or where it was coming from.

They will think it's a blight from God, he said.

The Senior Climatologist took his hand. What makes you think they'll believe in God?

He considered.

We don't, she said.

But they will.

No, she said. We *progress*. Species progress.

And this – her suggestion that belief in God was *regression* – this plunged the Senior Engineer into a despair he would not have thought possible, a year ago, before the spill.

The next morning, a crow alighted on the snow outside the kitchen. The Senior Engineer watched it through the window. The blue-blackness of it sickened him. The crow stayed a long time. It seemed its wings would never come unstuck. When it finally flew away, he turned to the Senior Climatologist. Will you marry me?

What the Senior Climatologist is secretly working on, in her lab, is slowing down the earth: slowing down the orbit, slowing down the wind, prolonging the days.

The Senior Engineer once told her, If the earth slowed down, we'd fall into the sun. Is that what you want?

As a child, she would step outside each morning and sidle up to the corner of the house where the wind was worst. The wind owned that corner – she had no rights to it – but she would creep up to it nonetheless, a kitchen knife in her hand. She would peek around it once, then step into the gale. Sometimes she managed a single battle cry before the wind made her swallow it. Choking, she would stab and stab and slash at its throat. How hard she fought.

On the following day, if it didn't show up, she knew it was somewhere, wounded, but recovering.

The Senior Engineer was preparing dinner one evening when his eldest daughter called out, for the second time: There I am.

He froze, the same spoon in his hand. He thought: It is happening. A rupture. A repetition. Two years almost to the day.

The Senior Climatologist, who was with him, set off for the living room. There you are, where? she asked.

There I am.

He made himself put down the spoon. He made himself roll his eyes. Here we go again, he said loudly, and the Senior Climatologist looked back at him, puzzled, over her shoulder.

This time, however, it was a siege in a Moscow theatre. Nowhere near the sea. The Senior Engineer relaxed. The government had pumped a debilitating gas through the vents. The rebels were dead, their leader slouched on the stage. The hostages nearest the vents sat stiff in their seats. Time had stopped inside the theatre.

While outside, it raced on. Survivors milled about, groggy but alive – the nature of the gas, and its effects, as yet undetermined.

His eldest daughter pointed. There. A young woman, supported on either side by soldiers, was trying to speak. The same Russian woman? Had she been on board the tanker?

There I am again, said his daughter.

The Senior Engineer and the Senior Climatologist looked at each other.

Wow, said the Senior Climatologist and sat down.

There I am, his daughter said again. Brain-damaged, but alive.

The wedding day dawned slowly, perfectly, pinkly. The Senior Climatologist looked lovely at six in the morning, and again at nine, and she was still lovely at two in the afternoon. When the sun set, she was magnificent.

As for the Senior Engineer, he soared through the day like a seagull. This marriage, his heart sang, this marriage might make all the difference, mightn't it?

Offshore, one mile down, the tanker held its cargo.

They stood beneath the wedding bower, awash in sunset.

The photographer, on his knees, was somewhere in the

foreground, sensed but not seen. An inky shifting stain. A finger pressed into an eyelid. Try not to squint, said the Senior Climatologist.

When the photographer said, Now hold it, the universe flattened and held itself still. Nothing breathed. Their hands, entwined, went pulseless. They became their photograph. Then something flexed and snapped back – they became muscular again – and the photographer, sensed but not seen, was saying, Good. Now I want you two closer together.

She was a little girl, blowing the night-white clouds out of the way to expose a universe so deep it was flat. She lifted her arms to it and said, Up, up, up. And her father, obliging, tossed her up to where she longed to go until she squealed with nervous laughter and he said, Bed time. It will all be there tomorrow night.

And she knew it would. Because the Senior Climatologist, even as a child, knew how to push aside the clouds.

Think of the power they'll have, someone had said, on her wedding day. She had heard those words, at the altar, just as she pushed aside her veil. Just as her new husband, for the very first time, tried to make a joke and said, Oh, *there* you are.

Tuan Vu

Michael says let's play a game. Write the first rhyming word that comes to mind when you say my name. I'll do the same for you.

I'm no good at these games. Bicycle is the first word that comes to mind, but it seems silly. Instead I write icicle. When I show him, he seems pleased.

What did you write for my name? I ask.

I think I've glimpsed the words egg salad on his paper, but when he shows me, he's written bicycle. I realize, then, for the first time, that our names must rhyme. This is portentous. This means I love him.

I love you, I say. I crawled through the fridge to find you.

Then I wake up.

I know why I dreamed what I did – the fridge part anyway – because yesterday, when Nadine was in the bathroom, I read the back of a postcard on her fridge.

July 10th, 2003

London, Trafalgar Square:

Here it is already halfway through our stay here, the days slipping by far too quickly. We had a reasonably successful visit to Alderley, though Claire refused to get out of the car when we visited the remnants of the old house and garden, saying firmly she wanted to remember it as it was and not to have a new image superimposed on it. She was and is still very much shaken by the near disaster of having her ceiling collapse. She was lucky to have escaped without injury. But the ensuing inconveniences, of which there are many, have taken their toll. She is very tottery on her feet.

Much love to you darling,

Me.

Nadine's fridge was magical then. Nadine's fridge was a portal. I put the postcard back under the Pizza Hut magnet. I did not think of Michael. Until I dreamed him.

I have lived in this tower three weeks. My apartment is two floors below Nadine's. Nadine and I met at the tenant barbecue. We were standing under one of the *To the 'artist'* signs, and she pointed and said, The first time I saw one of those, I imagined they meant me.

The signs, now posted in the picnic area, laundry room, and elevators, read as follows:

To the 'artist'. We don't appreciate your 'work'. We will find you, and when we do, you will be evicted. Management.

Like Nadine, the signs make me feel caught. They are a finger pointed at me. *Dear Management. You've read my stuff?*

Nadine is an older woman with soft, loose skin. I had her pegged as Australian, but in fact she's British. She makes window ornaments out of stained glass. Artisan, she confessed. Not really an artist. She invited me up to her apartment to see her 'work'. That's when I read the postcard.

When she came out of the bathroom, I didn't ask about Claire or the collapsing ceiling. Instead I said, So who do you think the 'artist' is?

No idea. You see my balcony is quite the showcase.

We were standing in a patchwork of colour, the light shining in blocks through birds and apples and hot air balloons.

Beautiful.

Thank you. She poured me some iced tea. She was travelling, she said, even if it didn't look like it. This was country number three. There would be ten in all. Ten countries. And she had ten years. A year in each country. She'd left England when her husband died. To travel, she said, instead of grieve. Sometimes you have to choose. She was progressing alphabetically. Chile was next.

I watched her over the rim of my glass. Either she was exceptionally brave, or she was running.

Where'd you come from? asked Tuan Vu the day I moved in.

Tuan Vu is not quite the landlord. He is not quite the maintenance man. He was repairing my deadbolt, rattling it, injecting it with oil.

Texas, I said. No, Newfoundland. The noise with the lock was distracting.

Which?

Newfoundland.

He looked up and to the right, as if to locate it on a map. New-foundland, he said. I was there on vacation once.

Did you like it?

He smiled apologetically. No.

That's okay, I said.

Too economically depressing.

I nodded. Did he mean *depressed* or *depressing*? Maybe it was the hotel, I said.

Abruptly, he stopped jiggling the lock. Do you play softball? he asked.

No.

He resumed. Too bad. Northland Apartments has a softball team. The Dragons.

Oh, I said.

Well. Maybe you will come see me play. The schedule is downstairs in the mailroom.

The mention of the mailroom made me think of the sign. Mr. Vu? Do you know who the artist is?

Ah. You mean the artist who is no artist? No. But we will catch him.

Where's his artwork? I'd like to see it.

That's pretty funny, said Tuan Vu, wiping his hands on his jeans. Okay. Lock's all fixed.

Michael lived, and perhaps still lives, in Houston in a gated community. That's not a euphemism. There really is such a thing. I didn't know that until he wrote to me. He'd just landed a job with an oil company. He wrote, Come join me in my gated community. You must be kidding, Michael. But then, why not? A writer can be a writer anywhere, can't she?

And I could have stayed forever. The gates closed behind me, the guards nodded and knew me. I could have stayed forever. Such is the power of admission. To be admitted, yes, is like being loved. A gated community is like being loved.

Michael did not, however, feel the cameras like a caress. He'd been there six months. One night, he danced in the streets. Not for himself. Not for me.

He said, I'm like Jim Carrey in that movie.

The Mask? I said hopefully.

No.

Ace Ventura: Pet Detective? I knew, of course, which movie he meant, but I wasn't about to say it. Oh no. Then the sky would start falling. I looked up.

Let's go inside.

We did, and Michael turned up the stereo, loud. Jazz. His feet made beautiful prints in the new carpet. He spoke into my ear. Remember that scene in *The Firm*? he said. Remember?

I shook my head. The stereo up loud so Tom Cruise could speak to his pretty wife without being heard – the whole house, the whole world, bugged.

What's wrong? I asked him. I was a fool.

I'm afraid.

I turned down the stereo. Of *what*? My voice was not very kind.

The sofa was so long it was practically a road. Michael sat on the horizon. Remember how you were afraid of perfume that winter?

You asked me to come here why?

If I could go back now, I'd crawl down that sofa and hold on to him. I'd make our names rhyme. Michael, icicle, bicycle, Brenda Sue. We can walk out of here and go home. Tom Cruise got away. Jim Carrey found a door in the sky. I'm afraid too, of being cast in, of being cast out – I don't know – afraid this is Eden, afraid this is jail. Not knowing the difference.

Instead I held my ground, held up the sky, locked the doors, unnecessarily. Nobody move. Everything's fine. But Michael found a door, a door of his own. One morning he was gone. And I was alone in Texas. What is Texas? I looked for it on the map in the kitchen but it was gone.

What Michael was referring to, the perfume incident, happened when we first started dating, in St. John's. It was January, and we were falling in love, and all I wanted was to be beautiful under my coat. To feel my coat fall away and be Venus underneath. I bought Allure, the perfume, at Shoppers Drug Mart. Chanel makes it. We went to dinner. My coat slipped nicely off my back.

Then I said, I'm wearing a perfume that millions have worn and millions will wear, and I feel connected to them in a not so pleasant way. Women have smelled this way before parties. Before weddings. Before sex. Women have been raped while smelling this way. They've been in car accidents with this scent on their wrists. Buried with this scent on their collars. I *would* get morbid. I'm sorry.

You might all be wearing the same shoes too, Michael said calmly. Or using the same shampoo.

But it's not the same as scent. Scent is like place. It's like we're all trying to live in the same place.

And this isn't a good thing.

No, it's scaring me.

Let's go home and wash it off.

So we did, and it turned out all right. Because that got me undressed, and him too, in the end – and not only were we beautiful under our coats, we were beautiful under our clothes. Under our skin.

From my window on the tenth floor, I can see into a backyard on Bartlebois. At the centre, amid the trees, is a large, red *Tyrannosaurus rex*. This is not your average gas-station-variety inflatable dinosaur. This thing is solid. The wind won't budge it. It must be twelve feet tall. Even from here, I can see its teeth, a mouth that divides its head in half, its little atrophied hands, poised and fierce.

A child comes out of the house with a bow and arrow. He hides behind the trees; he sidles up to the creature. An elaborate dance ensues. He stalks. He scurries. He shoots and misses. He risks his life retrieving the wayward arrows. Finally one finds its mark. It bounces cleanly off the dinosaur's chest – but not in the boy's story. In the boy's story, the arrow buries itself in the beast's heart. The boy sinks to his knees. He appears to be praying. He looks up at the sky. (At me?) His lips are moving. I imagine he is saying, *What have I done?*

Tuan Vu said Newfoundland depressed him, but likely it was just the hotel. I could tell him – though probably he has already guessed – how much this city depressed me the first three days I was in it. My hotel was in Motel Village, a community of hotels and motels and inns. It was called the Inn Between, which it was – the kind of place that pretends very hard to be kissing your ass – sewing kits in the rooms, *Globe and Mails* outside your door – while neglecting you in some fundamental way. For instance: an unreliable door key. One of those glossy white cards that's supposed to give you the green light. Welcome. Only mine didn't.

The day I checked in, I lugged my suitcase with its yellow *Lourde!* sticker around a walkway bordering the indoor pool area. My room was very far away. The air was heavy with chlorine. It was three o'clock in the afternoon. The sky, on the other side of the ceiling, threatened rain. A recipe for depression if ever there was one. The pool was empty. I made slow progress around the perimeter.

My door, when I finally found it, did not admit me. I sat on my suitcase and tried not to cry. Oh Lourde, I said. I'd given myself a week to find an apartment. A week in the Inn Between. I couldn't get in. I might never get out.

I found Northland Apartments the next day. Tuan Vu took one look at me and said, Move in tomorrow. Okay? I'll have the place ready.

My only complaint is the ceiling. The ceiling reminds me of a hotel. It's textured. It's the kind of ceiling that bursts helium balloons. I know there's a practical reason for it. Soundproofing, I think. Sound gets lost up there, bouncing off the white ridges.

When you have no furniture, you fixate on things like the ceiling. For the first week, I didn't have a bed. I was lying on the floor a lot. I was lying on the floor, thinking: What if, at some point, I need to bring helium balloons in here?

But then I dreamed myself small, flipped the room upside down. I trekked across a white mountainous world. Above me, a sky like grey carpet invited me to fall into it. After that, the ceiling was tolerable.

Tuan Vu is in the elevator with a can of paint. Don't breathe, he tells me. No ventilation.

Easier said than done. I push M and wait. He's painting over some writing on the wall. It's been there for several days. I've noticed it, but not really. A message for someone. *Turn right on Bentley. After two stop lights, take a right on Charleswood. Follow to T junction. Meet me at the corner!* There are other such messages around. But only now, seeing Tuan Vu with the paint, do I put two and two together. I point. The artist?

Tuan Vu nods. Don't breathe, he reminds me.

Well, that's disappointing. It never occurred to me that these practical directives in magic marker, having nothing to do with me, could be the 'work' of the 'artist'.

Why magic marker on a wall? Why not a note on paper. Or a phone call.

Meet me at the corner!

The artist who is no artist. What was I expecting? Something scandalous. And, if not scandalous, then beautiful.

There's a certain light in the afternoons that makes my living-room wall appear to have a second doorway. It's only a shadow. But I will pause a moment, halfway to the kitchen. I will wonder if maybe my apartment is a two-bedroom after all. I don't look closely at the shadow. I never approach it. I want to preserve the illusion that I might someday walk straight through it and discover the second bedroom of my one-bedroom apartment.

Brenda Sue, how old are you?

Why?

Don't be touchy. Nadine puts a baggy-skinned hand on my arm. It's just that sometimes you seem older than I am.

I look down at my own hands. What do I say to this?

Tuan Vu says you left your age off your tenant application.

Isn't my tenant application confidential?

Well, no. She smiles. I guess not.

I'm thirty-two.

Ah.

For a moment, neither of us speaks.

So what's Tuan Vu's story? I say finally. Who is he anyway? *Management?*

Nadine shrugs. For lack of a better word, yes.

I did not wake up in the gated community and find Michael gone, departed like Jim Carrey through a door in the sky. I did not go down to the kitchen and find Texas missing from the map. I did not wait around for days, weeks, thinking he might come back. Often I imagine I did all this because it hurts less. Odd, I know, but it hurts less to believe that I was left. That Michael left me. That I was happy and Michael was not. He was afraid and I was not.

But it was Michael who woke in the gated community, alone. It was he who went to the kitchen, the United States on a map on the wall, but found he was no longer in it. It was he who waited for me. Only now, months later, can I begin imagining this – and only a little at a time – because when I do, when I reconstruct these images, there is nowhere for me to look. No matter how new this city, how solid the walls and ceiling, there is nowhere to look that doesn't open up like a doorway the moment I think of Michael. Michael at the end of his sofa. Michael alone and afraid. Nothing rhymes with Michael. Nothing I can think of.

The boy is no longer killing the dinosaur. The game has evolved. Now he clambers up the long red tail, up over the bumpy back. Now he wraps his arms and legs around the monster's neck. He speaks into the monster's ear, fearlessly. It is beautiful to see.

The phone rings. It's Nadine. Today is the softball game. We're going to cheer for our team, to support our tower. There will be a celebratory barbecue at Tuan Vu's afterwards. He is a confident man.

I watch the boy slide down the dinosaur's back like Fred Flintstone.

Have you seen the dinosaur? I ask Nadine.

The what?

There's a bright red *Tyrannosaurus rex* in a backyard on Bartlebois. Silence a moment. I hear her balcony door slide open. Oh my.

I think it's stolen.

From where?

A hotel chain. Dine-O-Rama. I just remembered it.

In the lobby, Nadine is carrying two large signs that say GO NADS!

Gonads?

Go NADS. Go Northland Apartment Dragons! It's a legitimate acronym.

Sure.

I made you one. You'll carry it?

I don't know.

Oh, Brenda Sue.

Oh, Nadine – what?

I follow her into the parking lot. We're taking her car.

Nadine says, It's things like this, Brenda Sue. Carrying a GO NADS sign. I mean, what could be funnier. It's fun. It's funny. You need to – she's rigging up the signs in the back seat so they stick out the window – laugh a little more. There. Now. She hands me the directions to the softball field. You navigate.

I laugh plenty, I say. I look at the directions in my hands. Where'd you get these?

Tuan Vu.

He is the star of the show. He is all power and seriousness. He has organized the league, arranged the schedule, reserved the field. He is the reason we are here. And it's not just when he's up to bat, or when I'm looking out at the field, which is an odd thunderstorm green, that it feels like his place. It's when I look at the mountains – suddenly visible today, for the first time since I arrived. We're sitting in a purple-toothed mouth. A dragon's mouth. This is Tuan Vu's team and field and mountains. Just like the tower I live in is his, and the snow-swept ceiling, and the secret door, and the artist who is no artist.

After the game – a victory for the NADS, no surprise there – more directions are circulated, this time to Tuan Vu's house for the barbecue. He invites everyone, indiscriminately, tenants from both buildings, winners and losers.

You can be sure the Patricians won't show, Nadine says to me. Look at them. Sour grapes. Losers.

They are without gonads, I say. That's their problem.

Tuan Vu puts the directions in my hands personally.

Number 10 Bartlebois, he says.

Tuan Vu's nephew, Kim, introduces me to Thesaurus Rex.

Thesaurus Rex?

That's the kind of dinosaur he is, Kim explains.

Oh. I hear there's a dinosaur named after Alberta. Is that true?

Kim nods. Oh yes. The albertosaur. 1884. They found its bones in 1884.

You know a lot about dinosaurs.

I remember the year because it rhymes with the name.

I take a step towards Thesaurus, but Kim lifts a hand. Wait. I'd better tell him about you first. I wait while he scrambles up the tail and whispers something in the monster's ear.

He ate my whole family once, says Kim. I made him regurgitate. Okay. He slides back down. It's safe.

I reach up and pretend to shake the hard little red claw.

Some of the other guests have drifted over. Kim says, Halt. Stay back. Come no further, please. One at a time. Otherwise, too dangerous.

I find Tuan Vu by the barbecue. I put a finger on his shoulder. You stole that dragon from Dine-O-Rama, I say under my breath. I've had just two beers, but I'm suddenly brave. I'm a brave woman, it seems, in Tuan Vu's backyard.

Dragon?

Dinosaur. Whatever.

He leans in close. My nephew and that dinosaur need each other. That is all.

I leave my finger on his shoulder.

You're a thief.

Who is no thief.

So easy to be stuck, Nadine is saying.

We are the last to leave, Nadine and I. We sit on Tuan Vu's deck and his tower, our tower, looms very large, lit up like so many bright teeth in the darkness.

Thesaurus Rex hides in the trees. Kim had to go home. Before he left, he said, Do not go near that dinosaur without my protection.

Tuan Vu comes through the screen door.

So easy to be stuck, Nadine says again. Her voice is hoarse from having screamed GO NADS for two hours straight.

Yes, says Tuan Vu. You are right.

He sits down beside me on the steps that lead to the yard.

Nadine is behind us in a chair. I bend backwards so I can see her. Stuck how?

It's easy to say, The world has changed, but I have not. Will not. To stay stuck.

She is drinking something in a small glass, which means it's strong.

I remember the words on her fridge. To say, the gods are dead? I ask.

Yes. When it's you who are dead, she says. You who won't ride out to meet the world. You look for a way back – but if you found one, you wouldn't go. It's heartbreaking, but you wouldn't go.

There's a secret door in my apartment, I say.

What door? says Tuan Vu.

No door.

After a moment, he says, I came to Canada with so many pictures in my head. Mountains, towers, winter. I came and found nothing. It took me years to stop living in Vietnam, in my head.

The place where you are *not* always takes up more space in your mind than the place where you are. Proust said that.

But Tuan Vu says, That's not true. It doesn't have to be. For me, now, this is the place. *This* is my place. He lies back on the deck, content.

I want that, I say.

Me too, says Nadine sadly. And what are the chances that, in one of ten countries, I will find it?

I locate my dark window in the tower. I want my choices to have been the right ones. I want to have been brave, not cowardly. I want to be sure. I want, I want.

I want my name to rhyme with yours.

Cleave

He is a man who looks like Virginia Woolf. He is across the room and not quite laughing at me. I am in love.

We are at the York Club in Toronto. It's all so Victorian. Women are still only permitted through the back door and are barred from the room upstairs where the men drink brandy.

But tonight I sprang through the front door in my Napoleon costume, and nobody stopped me. It is Hallowe'en. Concessions can be made. Who would stop Napoleon? And now here is Virginia Woolf in the brandy-drinking room and I in the doorway, pushing my boot across the threshold.

Virginia crosses the room.

Let's blow this popsicle stand, I say – and when I say 'popsicle' something pops in his Woolfish face and he laughs, delighted, because I am such a breath of fresh air.

We do blow the popsicle stand, but first I must say goodbye to my parents. I find them in the dessert room. My mother is Anne of Green Gables. Every year she is Anne of Green Gables. This year her freckles are too big and too black. They look like my father's handiwork.

You've met Virginia Woolf, she says. And you're leaving early.

She sees everything, my mother. She sees through walls and even into rooms where she is not permitted. My father, on the other hand, who has permission to look, never does.

Who?

Woolf, Mother barks.

Father is not dressed up. I mean, he is suit-and-tie dressed up, but no costume. He looks me up and down. I slide my hand into my vest and stomp my foot a little. He shakes his head. You've met Virginia Woolf, he says, and you're leaving early.

It is always like this. My parents repeat each other, but they do not overlap.

Well, have a good time, says my mother, her words bright and orange as the braid she swings over her shoulder. Her name really is Anne. And she was born in PEI.

Yes, have a good time, says Father, painting the same words black.

Five minutes later I'm descending the stairs with Virginia Woolf. I march. He glides. He is tall and lithe. I am small and ridiculous. We are meant for each other. We leave through the front door.

Virginia Woolf drives a Jaguar. I stroke the hood ornament as I walk by.

Do you know why we love cats? I ask, opening my door. Because they are monsters in miniature. Our worst fears shrunk down to sit-in-your-lap size.

Virginia thinks about this a moment. I don't love cats, he says.

No?

But I do love cars.

He turns the ignition. We back out of the parking lot rather quickly.

When I saw you in the door of the brandy-drinking room, he says, I forgot what century we were in.

The York Club has that effect.

No. I mean I thought it was 1815.

Eighteen-fifteen?

The Battle of Waterloo, he prompts.

Oh right.

We turn the corner onto Bloor.

I don't remember the Battle of Waterloo. I killed a lot of people I guess.

About forty thousand.

Shocking.

Virginia gives me a schoolteacherish look. On the morning of June 18, 1815, it was raining, he says. Your musket was damp and you doubted it would fire so you kicked it into the mud. Ring a bell?

No.

You were hungry. Your white horse was dirty. The horse would be captured but not killed. You loved that horse.

And I loved Josephine. Thanks for the refresher.

Virginia Woolf is a good driver. He indicates well in advance. The cat on the hood points the way, and he follows. He and the cat are of one mind.

You never killed anyone, I say. Aren't you precious.

Except myself, he says.

Virginia Woolf flew in this morning from New York on business. Two women at his ten o'clock were dressed up as those conjoined twins from Iran. They'd sewn two wigs together and wore a white sheet draped over their heads. The others at the meeting thought the costume in extremely poor taste. The VP of distribution admonished the twins for making light of tragedy.

Virginia tells me this story as we cruise down Bay Street towards his hotel. He makes quotation marks above the steering wheel when he says 'making light of tragedy'.

One of the twins went home, he tells me. The other he found crying in the mezzanine, the wigs like a cat in her lap. He tried to console her. He told her he thought her costume showed imagination and was very much 'of the moment'. The woman stroked the wigs and said, But no one understands. I *loved* the conjoined twins from Iran. The night of their operation in Singapore, I kept vigil. When they died, a piece of me died too.

My costume is not of the moment. Nobody tells me it's in poor taste. I am not accused of making light of tragedy. But I am. I brush forty thousand deaths off my shoulders. I do not remember the Battle of Waterloo.

But I remember the conjoined twins. They were about my age. One of them, the one on the left, could actually drive a car. It was amazing to see. The way they slipped in, together, through the driver's-side door. And the way they sat, heads together like lovers, the passenger side gaping empty. They might have been lovers, cruising the streets of Tehran.

I confess I was disturbed, in those up-close interviews, by the way their faces stretched away from each other. It would never do to speak of this: How their longing to be apart had manifested itself in those features. But I knew, just by looking at them, how often they'd tried to walk in separate directions. The fury with which they'd sometimes attempted this. They were all smiles in the interviews, but their mouths twitched. Mouths that longed for just one effective aside. Not to be had. Not in this lifetime.

Now I tip my head towards Virginia Woolf. Who drives a Jaguar. A Jaguar has bucket seats. A console rises like a mountain range between driver and passenger. Conjoined twins could not drive this car.

He takes me to the lounge in his hotel.

So where's the mezzanine where the broken twin cried? I ask.

A different hotel.

Our table is a half moon. We are not across from each other. We are not kitty corner. We are points on a contiguous arc. The candle at the centre jumps when I breathe.

Crying in the mezzanine sounds beautiful.

But it wasn't.

I wonder what he means. I wonder what I meant. I think I meant only that it sounds like a love song. I don't think I meant anything more than that.

The tablecloth is white. So is the synthesizer in the corner with letters in gold across the front that say Katarina Bach. The woman behind the synthesizer is tall and blond. She's wearing the white dress Marilyn Monroe made famous. She blows into a microphone and announces that she is the one, the only, Katarina Bach. The words echo. The reverb's up way too high. We wait an eternity for her name to finish saying itself.

Virginia plays with his drink, pushing it away, then pulling it back, hand curled like a paw.

I ask him, Would I love you if you weren't Virginia Woolf?

It so difficult at this table to look into each other's eyes.

It was your bell curve hat, Virginia says, that did if for me. You don't know how many fools I've watched make Napoleon hats out of tablecloths. Promise me you'll never take it off.

Beneath my hat, I can feel my hair squished into unstraight shapes. I can't promise that.

Katarina Bach's name is finally over. She slouches into a sexy pose to reach the keys. She is too tall for her instrument.

She plays something unexpectedly complicated.

It's a fugue, says Virginia.

Whatever it is, it reminds me of my parents. It repeats itself a thousand different ways until the blackness creeps in.

I slide along the arc of table. I want to touch him, or face him. Virginia Woolf. Who drives a Jaguar quickly. Who finds a little Napoleon not unattractive.

Why did you laugh when you first saw me? I ask.

It was nervous laughter.

Because I've killed so many. And he's killed himself. And we must be prevented from doing this in the future.

After her set, Katarina sits at the bar with her back exposed.

She's a man, Virginia says.

I know. So are you. I've got it all clear in my head.

He puts a long hand over mine. There was a time when one was two. When we had two heads, four arms, four legs. Do you remember? We didn't walk – we cartwheeled. Also we had two sexes. Or rather, two sets of reproductive organs. Sometimes the sexes were the same, sometimes they were different. Try to remember. We were excellent cartwheelers. All-terrain cartwheelers, fast and powerful. But of course it was only a matter of time before the gods noticed and split us apart. So we couldn't cartwheel like we used to, so we'd spend eternity looking for our missing halves. Thus, the birth of love.

That's Plato, I say.

More or less. But Plato never meant that story to be the definitive word on love. It wasn't Socrates' story. It belonged some chump at the table who'd had too much to drink.

It's the only story I remember.

Virginia nods. I can never remember what Socrates said. He was such an ass.

So if the twins in Iran had perfected cartwheeling – is this what you're saying?

I'm saying, says Virginia, that we remember the story because we *remember* the story.

And I do. I remember her now, my conjoined twin. Though I never saw her face. I remember how the arms felt that were not mine. The legs like a dance partner's. How I never needed to look *at* her, or *for* her, because she was always there.

I would do anything, anything, to slide into a car in one fluid motion. Through the same door. To feel her on me. A shadow, an echo. Overlap.

I stare at Katarina Bach's broad lonely back. I hold on to Virginia Woolf's hand.

Aloha

Kathy's eyes have gone all pointy with worry. Mike rubs her back as they line up to go through security.

Kathy says, 'Did we mishear him? We must have misheard him.'

'Don't think so.'

They inch forward. At the last moment, Kathy snatches her cell phone from the little grey tray and steps out of line. 'I'll be thinking about this the whole time we're away.'

'Okay.' Mike would be happy not to go, truth be told. He is only now realizing how happy. 'So what do we do?'

'Phone the cab company.'

'All right.' He follows her to a quiet corner.

It was still dark when they got in the cab this morning. The driver was eating something fried. He talked all the way to the airport. One of the things he'd said, which Mike thought was pretty funny, was that all Stop signs should be replaced with Yield signs. 'Full stops, my ass,' he said. 'Yield is what we do. We're all about yielding. Slow down, look both ways, move on through. And yet' – he turned stiffly in his seat, his neck was very thick – 'how many Yield signs do you see out there? Precious few.' His voice went up a notch. 'We yield. Who the fuck ever comes to a full stop?'

Wow, Mike was thinking.

'Excuse me,' Kathy said, leaning forward. 'But I do. Especially in a school zone, I do.'

'Well la-di-da.'

'Whoa,' Mike said as they glided straight through a flashing red light.

'Look, she's in the minority is all I'm saying,' said the driver, who assumed Mike was coming to Kathy's defence. 'If there's nothing coming, there's *nothing coming*. Move on through.'

Mike and Kathy looked at each other in the back seat. Mike

wanted to laugh. His eyes *begged* Kathy to laugh with him – but she was having none of that. I'm marrying this woman, Mike thought. This is bad. Is this bad? He told himself to relax. You *are* relaxed. She's uptight. Whatever. It's early. Let's not be tragic.

And it wouldn't have been tragic, there'd have been no crisis, they'd have been on their way to Hawaii, if the driver hadn't said, just as he pocketed their fare, 'Have a nice trip now, you two. I'll take *real* good care of your place.'

'Excuse me?' Kathy said.

But Mike was slamming the door, hoping he was wrong about what he'd just heard, praying Kathy had heard something different, because if she hadn't, oh boy.

'Did he just say "I'll take real good care of your place"?'

Mike put the suitcases down. 'I don't know,' he sighed. 'Yeah, I think so.' He watched the cab pull away. It was 6:30 a.m. He was groggy. It had not yet occurred to him that this might lead to Cancellation of the Trip.

'Oh my God,' Kathy was saying. She loosened the silk scarf around her neck the way men loosen their ties in movies.

It's not that Mike doesn't like to travel. It's *Hawaii* – what's wrong with him? He's just one of those people who, in the final moments before any upheaval, regrets everything – his own birth, Kathy's, the very dawn. Mike always looks for a way out. Or rather, he looks for a way to stay put.

The taxi driver, bless him, may just have provided him with one.

Now, listening to Kathy on her cell phone, Mike's head begins to clear. That's right, he's thinking. We'd better not go. Who knows what that thug has in store for our ground-floor apartment with the window in the back that doesn't lock. Kathy's laptop is right there on the desk with all those confidential medical files she downloaded from work.

She was working till the very last minute last night. 'They'll never survive without me for two weeks,' she said, her eyes getting all pointy.

Mike loved her best then, when he saw that she was not so differ-ent from him. She was dreading this trip as much as he was. This upset to their *routine*. The difference between them was that Kathy got worked up – might even, very suddenly, burst into tears – but by God she carried on. She went through with a thing. While Mike, given the chance, would *not* go through with a thing. Given the chance.

The routine is sacred, Mike remembers thinking last night as he climbed into bed.

Now here they are, not just out of their routine, but out of the schedule meant to *stand in* for the routine. That one-day special sub-stitute schedule meant to get them on a plane to Hawaii. According to *that* schedule they should be through security by now. According to the old schedule, the original, which Mike misses very much, they should still be in bed. They should not be getting up for another hour.

'Yes, one of your drivers. He threatened to rob our home. No. I'm afraid we weren't on a first-name basis. Like I remember the cab number. No. But he was very large and very –' Kathy looks to Mike to supply her with the word.

'Scary?'

'Pugnacious. Of course I realize that probably describes ninety percent of your workforce –'

'Kath.'

'What?'

'What the hell is pugnacious?'

Kathy holds up a hand. 'He was eating fried chicken at 6:00 a.m. Maybe that narrows the field. No? What a surprise. Look, the man is probably *breaking into my home* this very moment. I'm alerting the police. I just wanted you to know.' Kathy collapses her cell phone into a tiny square. There are tears in her eyes. She really isn't such a hard ticket.

'Let's go,' she says.

'Home?'

'No. Hawaii. Fucking Hawaii.' And off she goes, her shoes clip-cloppeting across the tile.

'Oh,' Mike says, following. But he cannot, he will not, go through with it now. The trip was off. It was fucking *off*. Every part of him believed in the Cancellation of the Trip. She can't do this. Someone was breaking into their home. What happened to someone breaking into their home? He feels ripped off now because someone probably *isn't* breaking into their home.

The only thing left to do is make a bomb joke at security.

Ugly And

It was at Jane Price's party that John Bartkevicius began to think in terms of 'ugly and' instead of 'ugly but.'

Take these two sentences:

1. The hostess, Jane Price, was ugly *but* warm and engaging.
2. The hostess, Jane Price, was ugly *and* warm and engaging.

In the first, you might even put a comma after 'ugly' to emphasize that giant leap between ugliness and warmth. While in the second, ugliness and warmth hold hands like longtime friends. You see how the shift in syntax involves a rather radical shift in ideology?

So John Bartkevicius is somewhat remarkable in this. Because he's not a young man. He's an older man who, on more than one occasion, has used the words 'cult of ugliness' to describe the present age. Several years ago, he was even part of a group that lobbied the Tate Museum to exhibit more 'lovely' female nudes. All this is to say that John was an unlikely candidate for such a conversion.

Central to John Bartkevicius's conversion is his relationship to Jane Price. So let's begin there. He first heard her name six years ago when he was on the jury for a well-known and prestigious literary award. Jane's novel, *Ice Dancer*, had made it to the shortlist. John, shockingly, had not read it. He was supposed to have read all ninety-seven books and narrowed the list to five. He'd read ninety (and congratulated himself on getting through that many). As luck would have it, one of the seven he *didn't* read ended up on the shortlist. He couldn't very well make an argument against it, could he? Not without exposing himself. So he kept his mouth shut and gave *Ice Dancer* two thumbs up.

Why hadn't John read Jane's book? Well, he'd already read eighty-four when he came to hers. The last one had been about a figure skater who fell and was paralyzed during an attempted triple axel. John found this not so fun. Indeed he found it excruciating. So when he picked up Jane's novel (winced at her picture, rolled his eyes at the title) and read the blurb on the back (unbelievably, another novel about a paralyzed figure skater – was there no end to them?), he said no thank you.

After all, what were the chances that *this* novel about a crippled figure skater would be different from all the others? Although, according to his fellow jurists, it was. John had never seen them so unanimously in accord. Jane Price's novel was edgy, dazzling.

When asked for his opinion, John ventured cautiously, I don't know what can possibly be said ... that dear Jane Price hasn't already said.

Exactly.

It became for John Bartkevicius a perverse game to see how long he could 'hold out' against Jane Price's novel. How long could he deceive his fellow jurors, and later, the public at large? Indefinitely it seemed. Through two weeks of deliberation he sat smugly nodding, speaking intelligently about the other four shortlisted texts (all of which he'd read) and talking complete rubbish about Jane's. To his surprise, he found he was enjoying himself – and not in spite of, but *because*, he had not read Jane Price's novel.

He began, as I say, cautiously, with remarks like: At the core of the novel there seems to be an absence. Fairly safe, a remark like that. He then touched on the 'slipperiness' of the narrator. Also pretty safe. He progressed to the notion of 'life as performance' and the importance of falling/failing. And, in the wee hours before deciding the winner, he launched the incredibly daring: This novel is quite a departure for Jane Price – implying he'd read not only *Ice Dancer* but the entire body of Jane's work! – and how could they, the jurors, fail to reward such a bold literary leap? Jane Price, he argued, had succeeded where her narrator had failed; she had leapt and landed, stunningly, and with grace. A triple salchow of a novel.

Good lord. In the end, it is quite possible that John Bartkevicius was responsible for Jane Price winning that award. At the ceremony, when he finally met her, he'd practically forgotten that he hadn't read the book, so persuaded was he by his own rhetoric, so carried away by his own eloquence. He made toast after toast at the dinner and got quite drunk. Jane Price was ugly, he found himself thinking, but boy could she write.

She could? Alone in the men's room, he came briefly to his senses. You are a very bad man, he said, wagging a finger at his reflection. But so what? If he couldn't argue why Jane Price was any *more* deserving of the award, he couldn't argue why she was any *less* deserving either. All books were essentially the same. This he'd learned after reading ninety-seven – sorry, *ninety* – within a two-week period. They were all about crippled figure skaters. They were all the same bloody story.

And so years passed. It may alarm some readers to know that, during this time, John Bartkevicius served on many juries for many literary awards. In all fairness, it must be said that he read *most* of the books he judged, and that Jane's case was unique in that he never again presented an award for a book that he had not, at the very least, skimmed.

In the six years between Jane's award and Jane's party, the writer and critic did not meet. When John received an invitation to the party (a book launch for Jane's new novel), he considered not going. It was February. It was cold. The roads were bad.

However, it was in his professional interest to go. He put his boots on. Jane Price was a big name these days. Largely thanks to me, he grumbled, breathing on the frozen lock of his car door. And there would be other writers and critics there. He must at least put in an appearance. So he set off to Jane's grand house in the country – why couldn't she launch the book in the city like a regular writer? – blinded by his own breath in a car that refused to heat up.

There were four entrances to Jane's house that John could see (and probably five more he couldn't) – none of which announced itself as a main entrance. The overall impression was of lumpiness; 'interesting' offshoots and Escher-like staircases confused the façade. If you could call it a façade. Façades were flat.

John stood a moment at the end of a long driveway blocked with cars (his own was parked on the gravel road a quarter mile back), cursing the ugly author and her ugly house. How and where did one enter such a monstrosity? Finally he chose an entrance that did not require him climbing one of the frightening staircases. He proceeded carefully, hanging on to cars' side mirrors for balance. The driveway was, he thought, an ice rink. How appropriate. And so of course he must fall. And fall he did, just when he'd almost reached the house. He slipped (even managed an eighth of an axel) and crashed, smacking his chin against the ice and sliding directly under a red sports car that bore the license plate PRICLES.

Poor John Bartkevicius lay stuck under that car, slowly freezing to death, until some feet happened past and he called out for assistance. The feet belonged to a small-press editor John knew and his wife. Together the editor and his wife pulled John out, stood him up, and brushed him off. It's not so bad as that, said the editor. Your chin's bleeding a bit.

I'm bloody paralyzed.

You are not, fool.

But his little finger was badly bent and cut and surely broken. And his teeth felt like they'd been jammed a half centimetre deeper into his head.

They led John up one of the ridiculous staircases and into the house. (He was not paralyzed after all.) Which brings us to Jane Price – ugly and sympathetic Jane Price – who descended upon them like a large bird. My own driveway! Oh poor John. Poor, poor John. I thought we'd salted the damn driveway. She looked over her shoulder as if to accuse a negligent salter.

You did, John said. It's deeply embedded in my wounds. You salted.

She put a hand over her mouth.

Was she *smiling* behind that hand?

Come and we'll get you cleaned up.

John followed Jane to a staircase at the end of the hall. They passed two large rooms filled with people John knew and for the most part didn't like. He sighed. A fellow critic caught sight of him from the far side of a room and, pointing at his own chin, mouthed: What happened? John ignored him.

What Jane called her 'first aid' bathroom was up three flights of stairs. John, huffing, thought, it would be.

So you slid under a car? Jane was saying.

A car named Pericles, John said.

Pericles? She paused on a landing. Oh, she laughed. No. It's Priceless. PRICLES. Because of my name, you know.

Ah. He couldn't have been less interested.

They reached the bathroom, institutional green.

Now sit, Jane said, pointing at the toilet. John sat. Jane rummaged around in a cupboard and produced cotton swabs, alcohol, tweezers, antibacterial cream, bandages. We'll do your hand first.

So they sat, John on the toilet, Jane on the edge of the tub, his open palm in her ample lap.

She was wearing a dress with a cross-hatch pattern on the bodice that made John think she should be carrying an epée. *That* part of the dress was black and sort of silky. But there were many, *many* parts to the dress that had nothing to do with the bodice. The part where his hand was now resting reminded him of a Christmas tablecloth from his childhood.

Bent over his hand, Jane was mumbling that, given his reaction to her last novel, she wasn't sure she wanted him reading the new one.

Hm?

She looked up. Come on, John. Between us.

Her face was like a cauliflower. Precisely that colour, texture, shape. Between us, what? No one praised your book more highly –

It was damning praise.

No.

Jane sat up. The humour, she said. There was a sudden, un-cauliflower-like flush in her face.

The humour?

You never once mentioned it. Now either you actually missed it, which I find hard to believe – you are a very ironic man, John Bartkevicius. Or you thought my attempts so feeble that, out of charity, you decided to pretend they weren't there at all.

Oh Jane. What could he say? But I, *we*, gave you the award.

But you didn't find the novel funny, Jane persisted.

It's about a crippled figure skater, he said, exasperated.

Jane said nothing.

I don't recall the other jurists finding it funny either.

You didn't give them a chance, Jane said. I spoke to one of them later. Carolyn said she'd initially thought the book a 'riot' – her word – but after listening to you wax eloquent for two weeks, she attributed her first reaction to some perverse streak in herself.

Could this be true? Carolyn Spinski does have a perverse streak, he said. Anyway, you deserved to win, Jane.

No, she said, I really didn't. No more than anyone else.

Well, not any less.

She gave him a wry smile. No, I suppose not any less.

Ice Dancer was not a funny book, he said finally, helplessly.

Fine. Well, don't read the new one. You won't find it funny either.

She had moved on to his chin, was dabbing it with alcohol. His eyes began to tear.

What's the new novel about? he said.

Horse racing. A jockey.

Who falls and becomes paralyzed? said John tactlessly.

Jane straightened, a cotton ball like an hors d'oeuvre between two fingers. She regarded him perfectly seriously. Then, finally, her face cracked open in laughter.

John exhaled. You had me scared there a moment.

Jane was nodding, laughing, breathless. Finally she said, No, really, it is.

It is what –

About a crippled jockey.

Stop it, Jane.

But it's *very* funny, she continued. The rest of the world will think it's hysterical. All except you, poor John Bartkevicius. Which is why – she poked his shoulder with the cotton ball – you must keep your mouth shut about it. No accolades from you, *please*.

John stood up. His chin throbbed. He tried to feel offended. He approached the mirror over the sink. His face looked like a car accident. My God, there's a chunk out of my chin.

A small one, Jane conceded.

No, a large one. Look at me. There's a piece missing from my face.

Jane giggled. You exaggerate.

A dent, John said. In my face. Does 'face' grow back?

Over his shoulder in the mirror, he watched Jane laughing.

My profile, he said. Look at my profile.

They both studied his profile. Now the tears streamed down Jane's face. John was not laughing. He knew that playing it straight would make Jane laugh even harder.

Finally she got control of herself.

They stood a moment, looking at his reflection. God, I'm an ugly man, he said.

No, just dented, like you said.

Ugly.

Dented and ugly. Not quite lovely. There are worse things.

Of course there are, he said. Like what?

Being unfunny, for one. Being so unfunny that one fails to find humour in crippling accidents.

John lifted his hands in surrender. Okay. Give me the book about the bloody jockey, and I promise to –

What?

Read it, he almost said.

What?

Find it funny.

Jane flicked off the light in the bathroom. We'll see, she said.

John followed her down the stairs. At one point he stepped on the hem of her dress, which was dragging at least two steps behind her, and nearly sent them both careening headlong into the downstairs hallway. Fortunately Jane was quick to catch her balance. She pressed a palm against John's chest to steady him.

What an entrance we'd have made, she said, gathering up her train.

Probably we'd have been paralyzed.

She gave him a little punch. *You,* she said. And they carried on safely down the stairs.

On his way home that night, John thought: Jane Price is ugly and warm and engaging. And if this book – it was beside him on the passenger seat, *A Horse Called Superfluous* – turns out to be funny, then probably I'll find I'm in love with her.

And so it was that John Bartkevicius came to put those words together.

Some might fault him for not going further, for not losing the word 'ugly' altogether and seeing *beauty* in Jane. But when one finally comes to *ugly and* – and very few ever do – one has crossed a bridge and gone beyond beauty. Beauty is a stick figure, half erased.

Incidentally, Jane Price's novel about the crippled jockey is worth picking up. It's very, very funny.

The Plane Princess

Once upon a time, disembarking, she came across a flight attendant's silver smiley-face badge. It was lying on the floor of the sloping tunnel that connects plane to airport.

Check out this tunnel. The sun angles through the little square windows. It lights up the badge like an orange flame.

But before I get to the badge – more about the tunnel. The tunnel! As a discrete space, not just a transitory one, how do you rate it? On a scale of one to ten? Because for me, the tunnel gets a pretty high rating, *pre*-flight. Notice it slopes *downward*. Nothing could be easier than embarking. It's like downhill skiing. Your carry-on bag with the extendable arm zips past you. Let me into that overhead bin!

The tunnel gets an eight, pre-flight.

But post-flight, it's a whole other tunnel. Post-flight, the tunnel gets a two, max. Notice it slopes *upward*. Notice it is *not so fun*. In fact, it's a pretty bleak moment, disembarking from an aircraft. Your carry-on bag protests. The extendable arm extends further and further; the bag drags half a mile back.

Gravity sucks, somebody says in front of you. And you agree. Nonetheless you want to swing your carry-on bag by its extendable arm like one of those martial-art weapons, over your head, a giant deadly propeller, and take out some of your fellow passengers. Because the tunnel's unbearable incline is somehow related to the length of time it took them to get their fucking acts together and *get off the plane*. How long did you wait, half in, half out of your seat, with your neck crooked and your cheek smooshed into those buttons that you have never, *ever*, out of courtesy for the 'crew', experimented with?

But all that is neither here nor there, because now, in the upward-sloping tunnel, the smiley-face badge winks sunfire at you from the floor. You scoop it into your hand. It is slightly bigger than your palm. It is heavy. It is beautiful. It is in your pocket.

You've seen these badges. The flight attendants wear them pinned to neon green turtlenecks. They are perfect mirrors, the eyes and smile just slightly sunken, carved into silver. If you crouch down, to flight-attendant-breast level, you can see your own face in the badge, put your own eyes in its eyes, grin a matching lopsided grin. You've done this.

Two months later. I walk briskly down the tunnel. If possible, the boarding process is even easier than usual. I sail into the aircraft. I launch my carry-on bag like a javelin into the overhead bin. Then I wait. I let the other passengers shuffle past, get seated. And finally, when only I am left standing in the aisle, I let fall my black leather jacket (not unlike the ones issued by the airline, though mine lacks the logo) – I let fall my jacket from my shoulders and underneath, behold my neon green turtleneck, my smiley-face badge, my crisp black pants. Behold, behold.

Some brief confusion on the part of my fellow passengers. I watch their eyes uncloud as they make the adjustment. Ah. So you are –

Yes.

And their eyes lower. Respect.

Some not so brief confusion, however, on the part of my fellow flight attendants. Some unease, I'd say. Definitely some unease. I take my aisle seat. I am in plain view. They are watching me. They are talking amongst themselves. But they do not approach me. They do not take me aside and say, Who are you, and what are you trying to pull? They do not show me to the door. They do not shove me into the upward-sloping tunnel and say, Be gone foul impersonator!

They compose themselves. They bounce back. They do their 'cross check'. And we are in the air.

Next to me, an elderly woman plays solitaire on her fold-out table. Then she sleeps. Then she plays more solitaire. All this within half an hour. Time passes strangely. Finally she turns to me shyly, stiffly (her neck obviously giving her some pain), and, speaking into my badge, asks if I would mind getting her a pillow?

I yank off my seat belt. My pleasure. And I'm up. Checking those mysterious compartments at the front and rear of the aircraft. I find everything but pillows. I find three leather jackets *with* the logos on the shoulder. I find a Bible (yikes). I find silverware (knives!) from a previous era.

Tap, tap on my neon green shoulder. Yes?

I'm afraid you'll have to return to your seat.

Our badges face off.

I was looking for a pillow for the passenger in 16B.

We don't carry pillows.

I see. Of course I knew that.

Please return to your seat.

I make a small bow. And return to my seat.

I apologize to my neighbour. Apparently we no longer carry pillows, I say.

Oh.

It's appalling.

Yes.

Did you know, I tell her, those pillows are made out of dryer sheets. Bounce, Snuggle, and whatnot?

I always suspected.

You suspected right.

I would do anything to push the beverage and 'snack' cart down the aisle, to snap down the little brake with my foot while I serve tomato juice.

I'll have a tomato juice, says the woman beside me. And while the flight attendant is pouring, I take off my badge, breathe on it, polish it on my sleeve.

The flight attendant leans over me with the juice and says, her lips barely moving, Do you know how to use it?

Use it? I look down at the badge. What do you mean, use it?

She straightens. Nothing. She does the flippy thing with her foot, unlocks the cart, and is rolling on.

Wait.

Yes?

I'd like a tomato juice.

Oh. Sorry.

I repin my badge. I'm thinking it is thicker and heavier than it needs to be, this badge. I sip my tomato juice and wonder about this while the woman beside me plays more solitaire. She has less room now, with a drink on her table, and the cards overlap messily, threaten to flutter off the edge.

Here, I say, and I span the gap between our two tables with the 'In Case of a Plane Crash!' pamphlet from the back of the seat in front of me.

Thank you, dear.

You're welcome.

As she spreads out her game, I look down and see a card I've never seen before. It's a face card, but it's not a king, queen, or jack. The image is not stylized like the others, and the card is not vertically symmetrical – I mean, if you turned the card upside down, it really would be upside down.

What is that? I ask, pointing. Oh my God, what is that?

The woman looks up at me. The princess, she says. And she hands me the card.

The princess is more than black and red and white. Her colours are intense. She is dressed in gold brocade! She is standing in a land-scape. Behind her green fields roll and roll. Hearts tumble from her hands. She is waving at the card-player. Good luck! Good luck!

I put her down. Since when is there a princess in a deck of cards? I ask.

The old woman resumes her game. Oh – you can get them now with princesses.

And what's her – place? Her worth?

Higher than the jack, lower than the queen.

Makes sense.

Yes.

I watch her game. I keep an eye out for the other princesses. I find they are each slightly different. Hearts, diamonds, clubs, spades – the suits fall from their open hands.

I am sleepy, but I must not drift off while 'on duty'. The old woman has put away her cards. I read the 'In Case of a Plane Crash!' pamphlet and memorize the emergency exits. I do the gestures with my hands. Two in front. Two over the wings. Two in back. Then I put my hand over my badge – like I'm pledging allegiance.

Do you know how to use it?

I go to the bathroom, and once inside, I take a closer look at my badge. I put two fingers into the eyes. Maybe they are buttons? I talk into it. I say, Roger that. I say, Beam me up, Scottie. Nothing happens.

I look at myself in the mirror. I've never looked better. This colour suits me. The badge suits me. I lean in, and there, there – I have a dizzy moment because the mirror that is the badge and the bathroom mirror are engaged in an endless war of reflection, and the badge is suddenly a tunnel of mirrors, going back, back – *through* me. There is a tunnel in my chest. The badge is a tunnel to the inside of me.

I turn slightly, and the badge snaps back to flatness.

By the time we land it is dark. I look across the seats and out the window. On the runway, a little man waves a glowing pink light sabre, à la Star Wars. He holds it in two hands. He does battle with the Dark Side so that we may taxi safely to the gate.

I help the old woman out of her seat when the seat-belt sign is off. For once I am not annoyed by the ineptness of my fellow passengers. It takes them, as always, a dog's age to disembark – but now I am there to facilitate. I pull coats and bags from overhead bins. Items may have shifted during the flight! I announce loudly. And to my surprise, they *have*. That's not where I put my briefcase, says one man. Hey, how'd my coat get over there? I shake my head like this is a phenomenon I am all too familiar with. Little devils, I say. They grow legs up there.

Finally we inch down the aisle. The upward-sloping tunnel looms. I sigh. Two flight attendants guard the cockpit. They look at my badge. They do not say, Fly with us again. But they do say, Have a nice night. So I thank them.

I step out of the plane and into the tunnel and there, tucked in the little control booth area, next to the steering wheel (because you can actually drive these tunnels!) is the pink light sabre. It is not glowing. It is just lying there. I do not speed up, I do not slow down, I simply reach out.

And I swear, just like in Star Wars, it leaps into my hand. I hold it under my leather jacket. It is glowing now. Glowing pink and making a happy humming noise. I continue to disembark. The upward-sloping tunnel is not so steep.

The Loss of Thalia

Part 1. One of These Things Is Not Like the Others

I wore this dress – white skulls on black – to the wedding of the man I'm in love with. From a distance, the dress is busy but innocuous. Up close, it's kind of abstract. So you might not see the skulls.

It depends on who you are, what you see in my dress.

I left the wedding early and drove to the apartment of the man I am sleeping with. A jean jacket over my dress, the windows down. I listened to Frankie Goes to Hollywood from a CD I'd burned illicitly at work.

This man I am sleeping with, he loves me.

On the fire escape, I said, The only way to make this okay is if I fall in love with his wife. And that won't be hard. She's beautiful, isn't she?

He stroked my hair and shook his head, no.

No, she isn't beautiful?

No.

Let me see the gun?

There is nothing he wouldn't give me, no wish he wouldn't grant.

He keeps a gun in the drawer beside the bed. This man I am sleeping with *owns a gun*. Chunky, right-angled steel. It leans its weight into your palm.

What I loved about Charlie's Angels wasn't how pretty they were, though that was part of it. What I loved most was how they'd hide behind doors, a gun in two hands. How they'd hold the gun up like this, close to the face. Then they'd pivot around the doorframe. Elbows locked. Like this. Freeze.

It was beautiful, that manoeuvre. I used to practise it as a kid, over and over, my index fingers playing the part of Gun.

Now I practise it again – in the apartment of the man I am sleeping with. I leave him on the edge of the bed, the gun case in his lap, while I hide behind the bedroom door. I wait thirty seconds and spring out. Freeze.

He raises his hands in the air. He doesn't tell me not to point the gun at him. He doesn't say: *It's loaded – stop that.* There is nothing he wouldn't grant me, even this.

Would I let the man who just got married play Magnum P. I. with me and a loaded gun?

The man I am sleeping with knows about the man I'm in love with. We all three know who loves whom. There are no secrets on this front. We work together, for the same company – and though there is no love lost between the man I'm in love with and the man I am sleeping with, we can still hang out together and have a good time.

It's not a love triangle because there's a fourth corner. Marlene. Who also works with us. There *are* secrets on this front. Marlene is no Charlie's Angel. She'd be appalled if she knew about the gun. Marlene and I are against guns. We are against men who own guns. She doesn't know the man I am sleeping with is one of those men. She doesn't know I am sleeping with him, period. We are all *just friends*.

But the truth be told, I loved Marlene first. We worked together first. And after we'd confessed everything, everything but the very last things, I crouched down inside her cubicle. I had one last thing to confess. I'm bisexual, I told her – and it felt like a goddamn proposal because I was crouched so low in that cubicle, so as not to be seen above the half-walls.

She did not say, Me too. She is unhappily married, but not adventurous. She said, Wow.

She got a kick out of my crush on the waitress at the Mezza Luna. So did the man I am sleeping with. So did the man I'm in love with. Everyone loved me loving the waitress.

I was able to forget, during working hours, that the man I'm in love with was engaged. The fiancée (now wife) doesn't work with us. She's a respiratory therapist who hates smokers. I rarely saw her. But the wedding drew near. My love was a boomerang, always bouncing back. I grew tired and touchy. In a meeting, I called him a slacker, with the head office on conference call. Why hadn't he delivered what he'd promised? I meant a component of the new release, but I meant other things as well.

For two weeks, we didn't speak. Marlene was troubled. The man I am sleeping with was not.

I finally sent the man I'm in love with an e-mail. Meet me in a suburb of a suburb, I wrote. Okay, he replied. So we convened in a far-off plaza, a nameless bar between Office Depot and Pet City. There were Harleys in the lot, bikers inside drinking Rolling Rock. The man I'm in love with hummed that song from *Sesame Street:* One of these things is not like the others. One of these things just doesn't belong.

We sat across from each other at a table for six. I said, I treat you like shit because I love you. So I figure you treat me like shit for the same reason. Right? No response. I laughed. I finished my drink.

He went up to the bar for more. I smoked. It was Friday, a dress-down day. I was wearing denim. This boosted my confidence. This was going to turn out all right. I'd suggest the Nantucket Inn on the Boulevard.

He sat down with the drinks and accepted a cigarette. A victory, as I saw it, over the respiratory therapist. He exhaled and said, I thought you had a thing for the waitress.

Come on, I said.

We don't believe in the same things, he said.

I don't believe in anything.

Right.

Okay. I believe in things so I can compromise them. Case in point: the man I am sleeping with and his gun.

He has a gun?

Don't tell Marlene.

It's getting hard to keep track of what I'm not supposed to tell Marlene. It's like you're cheating on *her*. What's up with that?

I wish I was cheating on you. I wish you were mine to cheat on.

He was watching the bikers. This feels like a bad movie.

Why?

Okay, not a bad movie. *Your* kind of movie. What they call a film. Nonetheless, I said. You're the star.

A film doesn't have a star. A film is more democratic than a movie.

I tried to look into his eyes.

So the Nantucket Inn is out? I said.

God, the Nantucket Inn. With the whirligigs in front, and the waterfall?

That's the place.

As appealing as that sounds. He stood up, jangled his keys. Home to the respiratory therapist. You coming? he said.

I'll hang with the bikers a while. He was really leaving. Wait, I said. Invite me to your wedding.

What for?

Closure.

He laughed. Now we're in movie territory.

Cheesy is my middle name, I say to the man I am sleeping with. He rolls over, coming to my defence, but I shake my head, no.

My dress with the skulls on the floor. The gun in its case in the drawer.

Even when I smoke alone, I smoke for the camera.

Man, I can't believe I drove here with the windows down and 'Relax' pumping its cheesy bass line through my weakened heart. I can't believe I tried to send a message with my dress. I can't believe it didn't work.

Part 2. The Drill

This is the drill.

Mom calls at random. All she says is: Fire. I hang up. I start the stopwatch. I get the gun and shove it into my jeans. I go to the kitchen, open a can of Fancy Feast, call Tosca. When she comes, I throw the can into the duffel bag. She jumps in after it. I zip the bag shut, sling it over my shoulder. Out onto the fire escape. I shinny down the stories. One, two, three – the bag a live thing on my back. The last ladder unfolds to meet the ground.

Stop the clock. 3 minutes, 21 seconds.

I go back upstairs the conventional way, through the front door. I call Mom.

3 minutes, 21 seconds, I tell her.

Good boy.

We hang up. I let the cat out of the bag.

This is the drill. But when the phone rings tonight, I carry it out of the bedroom and say, No, no Mom.

Fire, she repeats.

Not tonight.

She sighs. In the event of a real emergency, you don't get to say not tonight.

I know. But I'm not alone. She's here. And she's finally asleep. She's had a bad day.

She knows the drill.

She does. But I won't wake her.

I hang up. The stopwatch holds its six zeroes. Not tonight.

Tosca, curled up at the foot of the bed, yawns *Thank you.*

She is in my bed, the woman who will be the death of me, her alligator back exposed. I pick up her dress from the floor – white mimes trapped in black fabric.

This dress distresses. I fold it, drape it over the chair.

I climb into bed beside her. I stroke her back. She turns. Fire? she asks. And I say no, not tonight.

She doesn't question the drills any more. When she's here, she takes part. She slows us down by about a minute and a half. We're working on that.

At first, she objected to Tosca and the duffel bag. She said, I have a proper carrier. Tosca is her cat, but she can't have pets at her place.

I couldn't sling a carrier over my back, I said.

She picked up the duffel bag, struck a pose. And it wouldn't look as cool, she said. A guy on a fire escape with a plastic cat carrier. Why do you take the gun? Really. Tell the truth.

Guns can go off in fires, I said. Under extreme heat. Firefighters have been killed that way.

She shook her head. I know who you're trying to be.

Who? I said weakly. Vance? Who else could she mean?

Can you see him packing heat, she said, a cat on his back?

Vance would never save your cat, I agreed. I didn't say – like *I* would. Like I *do*. I said, Then who am I trying to be?

Me, she said. You're trying to be me.

At first she thought the drills were a joke. She would slow me down on purpose. Undress me while I opened the cat food. Come down the ladder after me with nothing under her dress.

I tried to impress upon her the seriousness of the drill. I even tried to implement a fire procedure at her place. She wouldn't cooperate.

Then one night, on our way back from midnight bowling, we had an accident. It was my fault. But like I said, she will be the death of me.

We'd been bowling at Kazinski's with people from work. After midnight, the white lights went out, the black lights came on. Her teeth lit up her mouth.

She and Vance were arguing. The music pumped. We couldn't hear. He threw a ball over his head, down the wrong lane. Gutter ball.

His fiancée's eyes flashed violet. At me. So she *knew*. Only Marlene, best friend to my beloved, was still in the dark. Marlene, tallying up the scores in the booth. She was mouthing at me: You're ahead. You're winning.

Not quite, Marlene. Not fucking quite.

Because this woman, who will be the death of me, had just bowled a strike. She was strutting down the lane barefoot. Fred Flintstone in a dress.

Vance looked murderous.

He doesn't want her – not by himself. She would be the death of him too, and he knows it. Oh, he wants her, but with a chaperone in attendance. He wants her – *with* the waitress. He wants her – *with* the respiratory therapist. Maybe he'd even settle for me. Safety in numbers. A threesome, at the very least. It's so obvious this is what he wants. It's been obvious since that day at the Mez when she said, I'm in love with our waitress.

Vance Marquis is a coward.

He's getting married without me, she said once. That was how she put it. Then she went to the wedding after all – before she came here in the dress of a thousand mime faces, her own pale face like a standard on top.

The face that launched a thousand silent, wasted gestures.

But the night at the bowling alley was worse. She and Vance spitting venom under the black light. Duking it out.

On the way home, I said, My place or yours.

Yours.

Then she started crying. Vance Marquis, she said. Just his name. His full name. Vance Marquis. That was the first time I heard her say it.

She was crying in my front seat. She needed to hear Pink Floyd, she said. I couldn't take my eyes off her – she never cries – and I was fumbling with the CD – when wham! The front of my Acura crumpled up like tin foil. I'd rear-ended a sport ute.

I stared at the personalized licence plate: SAFE T. It was moving, or seemed to be moving – a mirage effect. Heat, I realized. Extreme heat. I sniffed. I jumped out and ran to her side. Her face was still wet. She said, My God. You hit someone. I undid her seat belt and pulled her from the car.

Stand back, I yelled to SAFE T, who was emerging, bewildered, from his tank. Stand back. She's gonna blow.

And this woman – who will be the death of me – she just laughed. Jesus, she said. You're too much. What is this, *The Dukes of Hazzard*? Cars don't blow. And *she*? *She's* gonna blow?

But then she did. With a sudden whoomp, up she went, in flames. There was something lethal in the air. We could all smell it.

SAFE T called the police from his cell phone while we watched my car burn.

After that, she took the drills seriously.

Now, half awake, she says, We have to find somewhere to go when the sun becomes a white dwarf. We need to plan ahead for such things.

I stroke her back, my fingers bumping down her vertebrae.

A white dwarf?

The reverse of fire, she says. When the fire goes out. Have you thought of that?

My hand stops cold.

We'll be dead by then, I say. Long dead.

Maybe, she says. But we need an evacuation plan. I was thinking about that, today, at the wedding, when Vance said *I do* in the church, and the sun went out. I thought, what if this is forever?

Part 3. Quincunx

Quincunx: An arrangement of five objects, with four at the corners of a square and the fifth at the centre.

Gun Boy was packing his weapon the night we took the Consultant to dinner.

I saw a flash of silver under his sports coat long before the Consultant proposed to Thalia.

When the Consultant proposed, I put down my glass and assumed a crash position in my plastic chair.

Marlene kicked me. What are you doing?

I waited a moment, then slowly unfolded myself. Dropped my napkin, I said.

Gun Boy was clearly in some sort of trance. I was the only one who noticed. The Consultant was looking at Thalia. Thalia was looking at Marlene. Marlene was looking at the Consultant.

The dinner was Thalia's idea.

She was bewitched (her word) by the Consultant. She said, I have no idea what he does. It's fascinating.

Apparently on the way from the airport, he had promised new icons. Little light bulbs that glow. Thalia nudged me. Because we *shed light* on your data. Because you'll *see your data in a whole new light.* Get it?

It doesn't get any more exciting than this, I said.

He's going to make us a dot com, she said. Be nice.

Then: Let's take him to dinner. Just the five of us at the Mez. So he'll get to know the Development Team. So he'll understand what we do.

What *do* we do?

She lifted her hands. Oh Vance. We shed light.

I remember Thalia, last New Year's Eve, belting out, I am not a pretty girl. That is not what I do.

We were outside Angelo's, waiting for the Drag Queen to drop. Marlene's gig. She runs a rock-climbing business on weekends. Occasionally she gets a request like this one: Can you lower me slowly from atop a six-storey building, in full drag, and make it so I touch down right at midnight?

No sweat.

We could see her up there in the spotlight, rigging up the Queen. Black sky behind them, their breath white fire. The crowd was screaming.

It's a song, yelled Thalia. 'Not a Pretty Girl.' By Ani Difranco.

I know that song, said Gun Boy.

What's your point? I said. I hate Ani Difranco.

They're going to play it, she said. On the way down.

Not exactly festive.

Appropriate though, said Gun Boy, his binoculars trained on the Queen.

She's *beautiful,* said Thalia, stamping her feet.

Looking up, I wondered who she meant.

The Queen touched down as Ani sang, So put me down, punk. The crowd went wild.

Over dinner, it turned out the Consultant was an amateur magician. One napkin became three. He pulled a fourth from Thalia's sleeve. A fifth drifted down from the dogwood tree. He confessed, I've done the odd show in Chicago.

Thalia was impressed. I thought you said musician at first, not magician. Vance is a musician.

Not any more, I said.

There's a piano inside.

No, I said.

We were on the back patio at the Mezza Luna. The waitress came with more wine and lit the bamboo torches. Thalia watched her.

When she left, Marlene said, Thalia's in love with the waitress.

The Consultant nodded as if this was just what he'd expected.

A magician, Thalia said, recovering. She turned to me. You see. He's more than a Consultant.

As if I'd been disputing the fact. I said, I'm as surprised as you are.

Do you saw women in half? she asked.

Yes.

This was unexpected.

How is that done, she said. No, don't tell me.

But we all wanted to know.

He said, You put the woman in a box, and you saw straight through the middle.

After a moment, Marlene asked, There are two women, right? Scrunched up in separate boxes.

Right, he said in a way that made it clear she wasn't.

His eyes were on Thalia.

Mine were on Gun Boy. I gestured at one of the bamboo torches. Isn't that flame a little close to the tree?

Gun Boy came to life. He got up to check. I followed him.

The flame is a little high, he said.

Maybe we should move it.

It was anchored to a moveable base. Gun Boy slid it sideways. I put my arms around him from behind.

What are you doing?

Helping.

Jesus.

I was frisking him. I had to make sure.

We returned to the table.

At the end of the meal, the Consultant leaned in on tanned elbows and proposed.

Marry me.

I assumed the crash position. Only Marlene noticed.

Thalia was laughing. You're drunk, and you're already married.

You remind me of my wife, the Consultant said. My wife twenty years ago.

Thalia looked down at the napkin he'd pulled from her sleeve. Then she looked sideways at Marlene.

Oh Thalia, I thought. You're a *sneaky* girl.

Because, predictably, Marlene came to the rescue. You smarmy bastard, she said and followed it up with, Consult me right out of my job, I don't care.

Gun Boy didn't move.

A week later, at the bowling alley, Thalia told me the Consultant had seemed more a template than a man. She had wanted to see the man.

Congratulations, I said and launched my ball into the gutter. You achieved your goal, though I wouldn't have taken a bullet for the experience.

She didn't know what I meant.

Gun Boy was packing that night, I said.

She glanced over at him. He was, of course, watching us.

Chivalry is shit, I said. And don't think getting it from a woman makes it progressive.

That is not what I do.

You want to be pursued.

No. I just want the templates to take on flesh.

And you'll fuck them, to that end, and be the death of all of us.

We were shouting. The music was loud.

She flicked her hand in the direction of my wife, my then fiancée. She said, It's no different from what you've done – what you do – with Miss Galatea over there.

Then she bowled a perfect strike.

I met my wife's family in San Diego, a year ago, when she was still my girlfriend.

The closest we got to Tijuana was the highway that takes you there and ends at a wall. Mexicans, I was told, were always slipping over, under, or through that wall. Some braved the ocean, then hit the highway, running. There were road signs – a family in flight, stencilled black on yellow. A warning to motorists, not to Mexicans.

My wife's family said, No, you really don't want to go there. Meaning Mexico. So we didn't.

I couldn't sleep in San Diego. The heat. In the mornings, I got up early and went to the beach. I watched the babes jogging, rollerblading, doing tai chi. They all looked like my wife.

This is where I come from, she'd said.

No kidding.

I'm a big guy. I'm in terrible shape. But one morning I got the urge to swim. I mean, really swim. I mean, to go south. I mean, to pass Mexicans, en route, and say, Trade ya.

I got out there, way out there, and my blood started up like a symphony. I heard this chord: E minor with a D thrown in. E G B D. The sound of a heart, overtaxed. A sound I recognized – and another I did not. A fifth note, coming straight through the centre of that chord. Not part of any scale I knew. A *new note*.

My wife, then girlfriend, was running up and down the beach, gangly as a horse. Vance, she was calling. Vance. Frantic.

I swam back. It was no easy feat.

On the beach, she put a hand on my heaving wet chest. She said, What were you doing? Where were you going?

Mexico.

You hate it here.

I bent over to breathe better.

We'll leave tomorrow, she said.

So what do you know of my wife, Thalia?

She doesn't inspire me, no.

She would never bring a gun to bed.

The closest she has come to malice was to say, *That cartoon dress.* Meaning the dress you wore to our wedding. It was her way of asking me something and still not asking me. I don't recall the dress, I told her. And it's true. What did you wear to my wedding, Thalia? A cartoon dress? A joke on your lips? A gun on your hip?

Listen. I can still hear that note – when I exert myself to the point of apoplexy. I heard it on my wedding day. But don't read into that. And I won't read into your dress. And we'll call it even, okay? We'll call it over.

Part 4. The Loss of Thalia

The Drag Queen introduced himself as Generic.

He said, Actually, it's John Eric. But it's become Generic.

On Angelo's roof, seeing him – *her* – in drag for the first time, I said, Your name does not suit you, Generic.

She stepped into the harness. It works though, she said, as a stage name.

Muscles bulging under fishnet. Big hands, shaking. Clip me in good now, she said. I'm scared as hell, to tell you the truth.

I looked at my watch. You'll be fine. Three minutes to midnight.

My legs are frickin cold. Why am I doing this?

To upstage your name, I said. To make tonight other than generic. I don't know. Ready?

Down she went, *Deus ex machina*. I am not a pretty girl. That is not what I do.

Twenty minutes later she was back up on the roof, spinning me around. You beautiful, beautiful thing! I lived! I lived!

December, one year earlier:

In the last act, Tosca jumped to her death – only to bounce back into view. Up she sprang, above the parapet.

A trampoline, behind the set. Thalia covered her mouth with one hand and grasped mine with the other. Oh my God.

With the final aria still stinging our eyes, we sat as if we'd been slapped.

It took a while to start laughing.

Then: She lives, Thalia cried, jubilant. She lives! She pulled me to my feet.

Now I ask myself: What does it mean, that a person can have two such experiences within a single year? Within a single lifetime?

Final glitch aside, Thalia said, did you like it? Tell the truth.

We were outside the theatre, wearing gloves. She'd let go of my hand fifteen minutes ago, to applaud the soprano at the curtain call.

It was the final glitch I'd loved. As for the rest of it, no. It was unpredictable. It made leaps I couldn't abide.

Still, it felt *familiar.*

We got in a cab that smelled of someone else's perfume. My transformation was almost complete.

So ended the period I call the Loss of John.

It began a few years ago when, in a split-second dream, I lost all respect for Jon Bon Jovi. Then it spread. It spread to all Johns.

There are so many Johns out there.

My husband's name is John. I use the present tense because his name is probably still John. And he is still my husband.

Then there's John Eric. Generic.

And there's rock sensation, Jon Bon Jovi, who took out the H to be less, well, generic.

Jon Bon Jovi. That idiot. I blame him for the loss of John.

You know those sexy dreams? The once-a-year variety that feel realer than life. And the next day you water-ski over the woken world, still in the dream's wake. I had such a dream about Jon Bon

Jovi. At least it began that way.

Jon Bon Jovi and I at a party. He says, Get me a beer. And I say, Get it yourself, stud. Clearly there is a spark between us. He confesses he finds me plain. Mousy. I point to my horse tattoo as proof that I'm anything but. He eats his words. We end up in the laundry room. We have sex, with me on top, really slow. Not a good kind of slow, but a ridiculous kind of slow that gives me plenty of time to look at him and think about his songs.

I'm a cowboy. On a steel horse I ride.

Man, that is brutal, I say.

I dismount.

So I couldn't love Jon Bon Jovi any more, and I'd loved him a long time.

I finally said to my husband, You gotta go. For a while. Maybe forever. The volume on my sex drive was turned down so low it was inaudible.

I told Thalia about it soon after I met her. About the loss of libido. Not the loss of John. I implied John was still around – but would rather not be. Unhappy spouses are useful. You can always invoke them in a crisis.

Do you think it was having the baby? she asked. Referring to the loss of libido.

I said I didn't think so. That was five years ago. The baby was no longer a baby.

Have you thought about leaving him?

No, I said carefully. No I haven't.

I really do have a tattoo of a horse. In the dream, he was still intact, his hind legs planted firmly under him.

The tattoo is just above my left breast. I got it in Milwaukee the summer I was nineteen. There was a Bon Jovi concert that weekend, and a Harley Davidson rally. There were lineups outside the tattoo shops. My boyfriend got the medieval symbol for quintessence – the fifth element after earth, air, fire, and water – tattooed on his bicep. I got the horse, rearing.

It didn't occur to me that my breasts would ever change shape.

Then, years later, I had the baby. Everything swelled and dropped. Including the hind legs. Now they veer off to the left like a spoon in a glass of water.

My horse is broken, I told my nursing baby. My horse is broken.

Thalia is connected to the Loss of John, though not responsible for it. The dream preceded her by a full year. But when I crossed the finish line into a new era, it was she who dropped a checkered flag in front of my eyes, she who grabbed my hand and raised it in the air.

I was different.

Oh, it's not like I went to the opera and emerged from the theatre Thalia-esque. Or like I started the rock-climbing business, dropped a Drag Queen, and found I wasn't so generic after all. But it went something like that. It really did.

Thalia. When she's shocked or sympathetic – hold on to your hands because she'll catch one in hers before you have time to lift it out of her reach. The first time she did that, it scared the hell out of me. But she has a way of making anything go. And by the time she crouched down in my cubicle and told me (if not in so many words) that she loved me, I didn't bat an eye.

The nineteen-year-old with a stallion *intact* on her breast might have.

But the horse was broken. I saw Jon Bon Jovi for the idiot he was. I climbed rocks. I dropped Queens. I'd had my hand held. I knew the loss of John.

She told me she was bisexual, and I said, Wow.

Perhaps this marks the beginning of the Loss of Thalia. In the parking lot this morning, I slapped a bumper sticker on her car: Charlton Heston is my President. She hasn't noticed it yet.

Where is the betrayal? In her loving Vance? In her fucking Jack? In her penchant for guns?

I already knew she loved Vance.

It wasn't at all like her loving the waitress. Her loving the waitress was like her loving me, once removed. But Vance hurt. Hurt me, hurt Jack – hurt her most of all.

The day of his wedding, to which (I thought) none of us was invited, I could think only of Thalia, how she must be suffering, counting down the hours. Why had we never spoken of this?

I turned onto her street just as she was pulling out of her drive-way. I followed her. To the church, the reception, and finally to Jack's. All day I stalked her, sweating in my car, trying to figure out what the hell was going on.

Now it was dark. I parked across the street. Under the fire escape, I strained to hear. I could see up Thalia's dress. Black spiders, white webs, repeating.

She said, The only way to make this okay is if I fall in love with his wife. And that won't be hard. She's beautiful, isn't she?

He shook his head, no.

No, she isn't beautiful?

No.

Let me see the gun?

They went inside. I sank down between two garbage cans and waited for her to leave. She didn't. The kitchen light went out.

The sky sparkled behind iron grid work. White stars on black.

What gun?

My butt was aching from sitting on concrete. I got up and hob-bled to my car.

I went back the next day, in full sunlight. Thalia's car was gone.

Jack was on the stoop when I pulled up, a duffel bag over his shoulder. He saw me, lifted a hand. I'd never dropped by before.

On the stairs, the duffel bag leapt like a thing alive.

He opened the door to his apartment. He put down the bag and let out a cat.

Don't ask, he said.

The cat licked itself furiously in the corner.

He? She?

She, he said.

What's her name?

Tosca.

She's not yours, is she?

Yeah.

Bullshit. What's Tosca then?

An opera.

By?

I don't fucking know. Look Marlene, what's up? Why are you here?

She's Thalia's cat.

Jack sat down, rubbed his face. So?

I know she went to the wedding, I said. I know she was here last night. I know she loves Vance. I know she doesn't love you. I know there's a gun. There is a gun, isn't there? I looked around.

Wanna see it?

Fuck no. What does Thalia want with a gun? Thalia hates guns.

No, he said. She doesn't.

Mid-morning, Thalia crouches beside my desk. She's been crying.

I take one look at her and sit on my hands.

How much do you hate me? she asks.

I shake my head.

Say something.

Okay. My voice shakes. I'd have taken care of Tosca. I'd never suffocate a cat in a duffel bag.

Thalia pulls one of my hands free and holds it tight. She says, It's okay. She doesn't mind. He feeds her Fancy Feast when she's in there.

Someone tall walks past the cubicle. Neither of us looks up.

I don't get the bumper sticker, she says finally. Charlton Heston. He was on the *Colbys*, wasn't he? Or *Dynasty* – some spin-off of *Dallas*?

He's the president of the NRA. Jesus Thalia. You can't love guns and not know who Charlton Heston is.

I don't love guns.

But she does. And she loves Vance Marquis.

I don't want to lose you, I say. What a soap opera line that is. It's not even mine.

But there's no time to try something else. The credits are rolling – right in front of my face. You know that feeling? When your time is up.

Go back. Go back to that first time she crouched inside your cubicle. Say something. Say anything. Explain the Loss of John. Prevent the Loss of Thalia. Say something other than: Wow.

Tell her.

Sling Shot Light

On their way downtown this evening, they passed an old church on Kensington. The sign said:

CH__CH.

What's missing?

U R.

Julia read it aloud to Marcus. He smiled. He'd seen it before. She turned in her seat and watched the church shrink into the frame of the back window. Dirty stone and dark windows. Then the spire pricked the sky, and she felt it, just for an instant, on the underside of her arm.

Who believes in what the spire's pointing at any more?

Not I, said the wife.

Not I, said the husband.

Though sometimes, if it's needle sharp, and if the sky behind it is the colour of blood, then Julia lifts a little at the sight. She considers what it might be like, not to enter such a church, but to scale it.

Julia and Marcus, in line for the dinner cruise, watch the Sling Shot launch another body into the sky. Julia feels each launch in her stomach.

It's a bungee jump in reverse, says Marcus, awed.

Nudged out by the Sling Shot, the Ferris Wheel, the prettiest ride there is, spins slow, mostly empty seats.

The lineup for the Sling Slot is longer than the line for the dinner cruise. The dinner cruise and the carnival are unrelated. They are two separate businesses. The Sling Shot and the Ferris Wheel are part of the same business, but the Ferris Wheel is the old guard and the Sling Shot is the young upstart. When they are dismantled and moved on to the next city, they will be shipped in separate trucks so each can pretend the other doesn't exist.

Julia and Marcus watch three 'shots' before their line begins to move. Remind me to tell you a story later, says Marcus.

For now they must watch their step. Up the ramp, then down into the glassed-in dining room. White tablecloths, candles, and outside, the carnival lights. They are led to a table on the shore side of the boat. A pianist plays in the corner.

Is he any good? she asks Marcus when they are seated.

Marcus waits a moment. Do *you* think he's good?

Julia doesn't know. But she pretends to consider. She lowers her eyes and assumes the expression of someone listening to – what? – jazz?

Then, tapping a hand gently against the table, she announces. Oh yes, he's good. He's *damn* good.

Marcus wakes to her presence. She can still do this, surprise him, delight him. He sips his water as if to regain composure. Julia, he says.

Julia is not musical. How many times has Marcus explained syncopation to her? And does she understand it? No. It's become a private joke between them, this thing called syncopation. Later, perhaps over dessert, she will ask him very seriously if he would mind explaining to her, what exactly is syncopation? And he will laugh, he will wake to her again, and Julia will have performed her magic, making the very thing that separates them their own.

For the moment, she says, You don't agree?

Well, as a matter of fact, I do.

Thank you. She smooths her napkin across her lap. She is pleased by how large it is, this napkin, the way one is pleased in a hotel to unfold a towel and find it continues unfolding.

She looks up and he is still watching her. Happy anniversary, Julia.

On the shore, a small shape leaps into the sky.

The ship begins its slow crawl upriver. Julia is facing forward, Marcus backward. The floor tips slightly as if on a thick stem.

You were going to tell me a story, Julia says.

Marcus nods. Well, not a story really. Something I heard on the radio. There's this guy at Cambridge who's researching a correlation between vertical transportation and vertical transportation. The physical kind versus the spiritual kind. In a nutshell, are you more likely to experience an epiphany, a sublime moment, a miracle – call it what you will – while *rising*, while aloft?

Julia laughs.

But Marcus is speaking in paragraphs. He only speaks in paragraphs when it matters. Of course, he says, Dr Bernheimer – that's the guy at Cambridge – *has* found a correlation. You are seventy-five percent more likely to experience an epiphany while rising – in an aircraft, say, or in an elevator.

Bunk, says Julia.

Silence a moment. Then Marcus says: Or, say, on the Sling Shot.

Bunk, says Julia again. The word 'bunk' is the ugliest word she knows. It falls like an axe into any conversation. She wants to stop using it, forever.

She pokes his arm and tries to make a joke. Just what kind of experiences have you been having in elevators?

Marcus smiles, looks out the window. The tension, and really there was very little, dissipates. Look, he says.

And there, on the shore, not a quarter mile from the original, is another Sling Shot, a smaller version. A red sign flashes Sling Shot *Light*. As they watch, a slightly obese figure swings about ten feet in the air then back down again.

The waiter arrives. Julia orders cold soup to start. Then the lamb. Or the salmon. Already she can't remember what she ordered. She is worried and can't pinpoint the cause. It's like going upstairs for something with your coat on, something you mustn't leave the house without, only to stand still, unsure which room to go into, unsure what you need, only knowing you need it.

It might be the pianist – he might be the problem. Or it might be Marcus's story, which was not a story. It might be that a new space has just opened up between them, dreamt up by a man at Cambridge, just when Julia thought she had all the spaces accounted for.

Or it might be that she is remembering all the times they have flown together, she and Marcus. And how silent they are, always, when the plane takes off.

Years ago, Julia took an empty train into the city. The train was silver. The sky was pink. And she was keenly aware of the train from the outside, how it must look, the sky being carried away in a mirror.

She'd been at a garden party and left early. There, under a tree that buzzed with some unseen insect, she'd longed for her whole life in one swallow. She wanted a thousand such parties under her belt. How she envied, suddenly, the hostess, Mrs Escott, with four grown daughters and a long-legged son. When Mrs Escott straightened her arm, her elbow collapsed into soft folds. Julia wanted that elbow. At night, in bed, she wanted to straighten one arm and feel the soft puddle of skin, emptied of bone.

And to think about her adult daughters and wonder, what will they do tomorrow and the next day and the next? And her one son, with long legs, with a face like that famous novelist's, long and serious, and who, because she, his mother, always said he resembled the author, will not read one – not one – of his books. Never mind. He has a girlfriend now, taller than him, whom he brought to the party and whose sundress, when the sun shines through it, shows her legs and, goodness, her whole body, in silhouette.

Mrs Escott had unbent an elbow and reached across the long afternoon to shake the girl's hand.

All this Julia was fleeing, or chasing, on a train in the setting light. There was a billboard, a sad young woman in her underwear, cradling her own naked elbows in her palms. Julia wanted to be old, not young.

The train seemed to be sliding downhill, but in fact it was just rounding the curve of the earth.

She married the long-legged son.

In bed, she would lift her naked arm, balance it on her shoulder, feel the *physics* of her arm, supporting the weight of a single finger, pointing.

While Marcus ran his own finger from her shoulder to elbow to wrist and back again.

The soup is cold, but Marcus is sweating. There's an unhealthy sheen on his face. He puts down his spoon. You're not feeling well, Julia says.

'Fraid not.

Julia nods. It's because you're facing backwards, she says, with your back to the motion. Let's switch.

Do you mind? But already he is standing, bringing his napkin and soup bowl with him.

Of course not.

Then the miracle happens. It lasts twenty seconds. When Julia sits in Marcus's place on the other side of the table, the pianist's music arranges itself in her mind like algebra, working itself out, effortlessly.

Syncopation, she murmurs.

Ah, says Marcus happily. He feels instantly better. Would you like me to explain it?

Would you?

Because already the music is tumbling over itself, waves overlapping, so that she is confused and alone again on her side of the table, not his.

Taxation

The other day, on lunch break, Steve was standing near the edge of the roof, and he said: Dan, sometimes I wonder what I'd say if she looked up here and asked me, Why are you up there, tarring the roof of the taxation centre? I mean, *why?*

I was trying to eat my sandwich without touching it. Because it needs it?

That was all I said to Steve, but I got up and went to the edge and looked down. In my head I answered her: Hey lady. Say it's my job. Say I have a few kids. Say this pays something. Say it's over at four, and I can go home. By four-fifteen I'm home. While you taxation drones work till six – even later now that it's springtime. You take your work home with you too, I bet, read taxation 'philosophy' deep into the night. Whereas I'm home at four-fifteen. By four-thirty I've got my before-dinner beer on the go. I spend the whole day outside, while under my feet, you compute my taxes. I'm up here with the wind, and a view, and a spring suntan to boot.

Does that answer your question?

On the weekends, I look pretty good. I'm showered. I'm tar-free. I'm in a white T-shirt and jeans. Tanned, like I said.

How long will this job last? my girlfriend, mother of my kids, asks me.

Oh baby, roofs don't get any bigger than this.

It's just me and Steve up there, slathering it on. Steve lives a couple of blocks away, and I've got him walking to work now, since the taxation centre's pretty close by. I call him up at 7:10 a.m. and say, I'm leaving now.

And we've got it timed so perfect that when I hit Liverpool and Hamel, he hits Hamel and Liverpool, and we kind of merge together like two rivers and walk the rest of the way together.

Steve needs the exercise. He's pretty chunky, and I keep telling him, if he doesn't take some off, he's never going to attract the attention of that swift little taxation hottie who goes out running every lunchtime. I use her as an incentive, see. But really I'm looking out for Steve's heart – his physical heart, I mean. Tarring roofs is not like shovelling snow, but you do it for longer, in the heat, and it's something fat people probably shouldn't do. So I dangle the taxation chick like a carrot, and I tell him to lay off the chips – and now, what with all the walking to and fro, things are looking up for Steve.

Things, but not women. Not that particular woman anyway. She never looks up. Doesn't know we're alive. No fault of hers, I guess. Who thinks to look up at the roof of the taxation centre? Unless we're at the edge, no one can see us anyway. It's like a frickin parking lot up there. But right at noon, count on Steve to be at the edge. It's heartbreaking. Sometimes he looks so desperate I think he's going to jump. Then I'll say, Back away from the edge now, Steve. You'll be even less attractive with two broken legs. Making a joke out of it, like.

How does she do it, he'll ask me. Meaning, how does she run without stopping, for a whole forty-five minutes.

She's in shape. You could be too.

Can you run that long, Dan?

I tell him no, but I'm one hell of a sprinter.

I invite Steve over every Friday night. Calie doesn't mind because I go home every other day and tell her all about poor love-struck Steve, how he's got it bad for the taxation chick who never looks up, and I've got her feeling so sorry for him that she's practically adopted him.

So Steve and me hang out on Friday nights, usually in the back yard, if the weather's halfway decent, because Steve smokes (his heart, his heart), and I won't have him smoking in the house with Calie and the kids. I've got lungs to protect, my own included.

This Friday night, though, it's raining, and Steve keeps getting up from the table, where the three of us and Amanda, my oldest, are playing euchre, and going out back for a cigarette. One out of every three smokes, I join him. Keep him company. That's my policy. It's a pain in the ass, leaving a warm kitchen, putting on my windbreaker, standing out in the rain. But one out of every three times is only good manners, I figure. So I do it.

We're standing out there in the rain, around midnight, when Steve says, I've been thinking, Dan, about maybe taking our lunches down to the ground, you know sitting on one of those benches.

Well praise God, I say.

He looks at me. What's that supposed to mean?

It means you're finally gonna to let her see you. I clap him on the back. You're putting yourself in her line of sight.

Yeah, he says. Hopefully I won't be blocking it completely.

Now, now, I say. This is very good news. I breathe in the clean moist air. You gotta give up smoking, Steve. You gotta give up smoking and chips. And you gotta walk more. A new leaf, my friend. A new leaf.

Steve drops his cigarette butt into an empty beer can. Maybe if she's worth anything, he says, she should just take me as I am.

What kind of talk is that? I ask him.

'Take Me As I Am.' It's a song by Faith Hill. Steve's crazy about Faith Hill.

I know. But the world doesn't work like that.

What about you and Calie?

What about us? It's not the right attitude to take with you, I tell him, down to that park bench. You put yourself in her line of sight with that maybe-she's-not-worth-anything chip on your shoulder – she'll smell it, a mile off.

Maybe you're right, he says. But I get down, thinking about it. It all feels pretty unlikely.

What does?

That anything could ever happen for me. Like you and Calie. Amanda and Josie and you and Calie.

A family, I say. Man, Steve. I wish I could just make it happen for you. I wish I could. But you've got a work at it.

Would Calie love you if you looked like me?

Let's ask her.

No, please.

I want you to picture this, I say, spreading my arms wide. Picture a barbecue right here in this very yard, a sunny afternoon, my family and yours – you and Taxi and your four kids.

Don't call her Taxi.

I'm just trying to get you to think positive. Imagine it in your head. Then make it real.

Yeah, Steve says. He's staring at the backyard, seeing that barbecue. So Monday? he says. Lunch on the bench.

You're on, I say.

I tell Calie in bed: Steve's making a move.

On the runner?

Yep. Monday we're eating lunch on a bench.

On the ground?

They don't have benches on the roof, love.

She jabs me in the ribs. Oh, I wish I could be there. She'd better not be snooty.

He probably won't talk to her, so we won't know.

Oh you'll know. You'll see her up close. You'll know just by how she looks.

Now, I say. Calie tends to be quick to judge.

I know. But a runner, she says.

Taxation, I say.

Monday dawns bright and beautiful, and I'm feeling good about our prospects. When I meet up with Steve at Liverpool and Hamel, he looks defeated already. I say, Don't even start. Today's the day.

I've been thinking. Maybe I should lose some more weight first.

I say, Look. It's a big roof, Steve. And sure, we can drag out this project a little. I'm willing to do that for you. We're buds. But eventually our work there will be done, and you may not have such a great view from the next roof we tar.

He nods. Point taken. But Jesus I'm a wreck.

You're just putting yourself in her line of sight, I remind him. That's step one. Just step one today. Worry about step two tomorrow. You just gotta sit there on the bench and eat your carrot sticks.

I'm pretty sure Steve didn't pack carrot sticks for lunch, but I'm always on the job, using the power of suggestion, as it's called.

At high noon, we descend from the roof and Steve skitters over to the little pond to wash his hands, while I keep watch. 12:05 she'll be out that door. You can set a clock by her.

Steve's got his bench all picked out, so we head over there, briskly. I've never seen Steve walk so fast. I hope no one's watching from those pink-mirrored windows, seeing two grown men hurry to a park bench. Who does that?

We sit down. Steve arranges himself. He *has* packed carrot sticks for lunch. I'll be damned. I pat his shoulder to show my approval. I can't talk to him right now. He's too nervous. I respect that.

We sit in absolute silence and wait. 12:06. She comes bouncing down the sidewalk. She's pretty damn lovely, I have to admit. Her eyes are pointing straight ahead, but wait, now they're turning, they're snagging on these two unexpected figures – who are these tar-splattered hunks? – on a usually empty park bench. What have we here, her eyes say, and they're smiling. I smile back. I want to congratulate Steve right there and then on his good taste. Not an ounce of snootiness. I can't wait to tell Calie.

Hey, Steve says. And he's standing up. His carrot sticks tumble, not a bite out of any of them, to the sidewalk. This was not part of the plan. Wait, he says.

She stops and turns around.

Step one, I whisper.

I tar the roof, he says.

I make a throat-cutting gesture. It's all over.

What roof, she says.

Yours, says Steve. That one.

She looks up. Oh yeah?

I see you from that roof every day.

I groan. I can't watch this. I put my face in my hands.

She doesn't say anything, and for a moment I wonder if she's gone.

Then I hear Steve: See, we're almost done here, and I likely won't be able to see you from the next roof we tar, like Dan says.

I sneak a peek at her, wave a little wave. Dan, I say. Nice to meet you.

Her eyes lock back on Steve. And you are … ?

So in love with you.

I start laughing then. This is too wild. This is too much. I can't stop.

Make yourself scarce, Dan, says Steve. Real authoritative like. Wow, I can't believe it. I'm embarrassed for him, but proud too. Real proud. Wow. I make a beeline for the pond.

It feels like I'm there by myself for a long time. I get myself under control.

I see Steve's squat noon shadow on the grass before I see him. I'm afraid to look at him.

We're going out Friday, he says.

I look up then, and he's smiling.

No shit?

No shit.

I let out a whoop and start doing a little dance, right there by the pond. Steve puts a hand on my shoulder. You're embarrassing me, he says.

The next day, Tuesday, I ask if we're eating lunch on the bench. No, he says.

At noon, he assumes his usual spot on the edge of the roof, and I stand there with him, watching. This I have to see. At 12:05, Mona, that's her name, comes through the east exit and the first thing she does is look up. She looks up and waves and Steve waves back.

Man, that is beautiful, I say. And I mean it, I don't think I've ever seen anything so beautiful in my life. I'm choked up.

Yesterday, after you got hysterical and had to go stand by the pond, Steve says, you know what she said?

I hope that handsome man is all right?

No. I don't think she noticed you were gone, to tell you the truth.

Okay, so what'd she say?

She said, What are you, some kind of angel? Like I'd answered her prayers or something.

Milaken

Tad reads in the paper about a lone hiker in a remote part of Utah who got his arm caught between two boulders and, after five days of trying to dislodge it, finally sawed off the arm with a pocketknife. Then he walked six miles back to civilization.

There are two pictures of the hiker, one taken before the tragedy, with two arms, and one taken after, with one. In both pictures, he is smiling.

This scene, the boy trying to free his arm, the decision, finally, to saw it off, the slow cutting, the eventual snap of that last bit of bone, the arm left behind between rocks, the torn sleeve wagging in the wind – all this plays and replays, is the background to Tad's day, as he goes about his work, feeds the horses, checks the fencing, cleans the house in preparation for the arrival of his daughter tomorrow.

Pray God Milaken never has to cut off her own arm, tethered to one of those mountains she is always climbing.

When she was little and had growing pains in her legs, she would sometimes say, Make them stop. Stop me growing. And once, when he woke her up to see the eclipse of the moon, she started screaming, said the moon was being mean to her, and her hands felt huge. Said: Cut them off. She'd had a fever, but Tad was really shaken. Cut them off, she ordered him.

Every night, Tad walks the circumference of his property. He walks clockwise, and at eight o'clock – in space, that is, not in time, eight o'clock on the dial that is his property – at eight o'clock, a spider drops from a certain tree, lands on his shoulder, and rappels the rest of the way to the ground. It reminds him of his daughter.

Hello Milaken, he says. He says hello to the spider as if it were his daughter. What harm? Tomorrow she will be here. With her friends. Perhaps they will all walk this circle together, after dinner, and he'll explain how his property is a steering wheel, how he travels too, in his way, how he's driving this piece of land through space – and he'll point out the markers. Two o'clock. Five o'clock. Eight o'clock. Milaken meet Milaken.

Tad knows repetition is a kind of erasure. What he will remember, in the end, are the things he has never repeated. The unrepeatable things. How many of those are there? How many days has he lived that could be the same day?

If it were him, shackled to the rocks in Utah, would he take the initiative to cut himself free? Likely not, no. He'd fast develop a routine with that rock. He'd love the rock very quickly. That is how he is. He would sleep standing, his right cheek pressed against the cold surface, and soon it would seem he had always slept thus.

But to begin cutting himself free, to leave an entire arm behind and walk away. An unrepeatable act.

These are your options: Either you cut off your arm, and time divides, here, now, into pre and post. Or you love the rock. You make the rock big enough to be your whole life.

You can either be like Tad. Or you can be like his daughter.

After he walks the circle, he returns to the house and watches *Home Crusader* at nine o'clock with Kent Snively. A traumatic half hour, one that Tad dreads but must endure. Kent Snively travels around the Midwest in search of structurally unsound houses and botched renovations – many of which Tad fears he may have had a hand in, twenty or so years ago. The Home Crusader peels back walls, tears up floors, has a terrifying knack for sniffing out cut corners – then brings the camera in for a closer look. Tut, tut, tut. Will you look at this. A fire hazard. An accident waiting to happen. It's a miracle the house is standing. It's a miracle you're all not dead. But in half an hour, he's fixed it all, tipped his hat, and is gone. The Home Crusader at your service.

Watching *Home Crusader* is Tad's penance for all the shoddy work he's ever done. He waits to hear Kent Snively say it: This has Tad Wilkins written all over it. A Tad Wilkins special right here.

Now Tad breeds horses and grows corn. The last thing he built was this house. And here, he cut no corners. That he knows of. Problem is, there are always corners Kent Snively knows about that nobody else does.

Tad built the house at exactly twelve o'clock – in space, that is, not time. Though, oddly, he remembers the moment the house felt truly finished, and that was at high noon on a Tuesday. Anyway, he did a good job on this house. As far as he can tell. And on the barn too, which stands at three o'clock.

When *Home Crusader* is over, and his name hasn't been mentioned, Tad celebrates by heating up some of this morning's coffee and a piece of pie. He used to keep well back from the microwave while it did its business. But ever since Milaken got him the book *Risk: A Practical Guide for Deciding What's Really Safe and What's Really Dangerous in the World Around You,* Tad stands in close, like the microwave's a personal friend, whom he trusts.

The book proclaimed the appliance safe, so now Tad and the microwave are buds. But it's more than that. There are certain objects in the world Tad recognizes as keys – there's no other word for them. They offer a solution to something. They could unlock this space he's living in, if he knew how to use them.

When something is heated, the book explained, its molecules move faster. Cause and effect. That's why water jumps around when it boils. How the microwave works, as Tad understands it, is by reversing that process. The microwave jiggles the molecules and says: Let there be heat. *It flips cause and effect.* This means something. How can it not mean something? This little equation, if it could be applied to other things, could make the impossible possible. Or so Tad senses.

There are other keys. A horse's eye. The oblong pupil that stays wide even in sunlight, with some kind of stalactite formation in there. The eye Tad quit construction for. There's a landscape in that eye, so clear you think it must be reflecting the place you're standing in, but then you look around you, and the world is nothing like that.

Or the Grand Canyon – the one time Tad was there. You feel it before you see it. You drive along this road, with trees between you and it, so you don't know it's even there, at first. But all the while there's this hollow feeling in your chest, on the *right* side of your chest. And then something makes you look to your *right,* the trees give way – and what the hell is that? The answer.

If you could flip cause and effect. If you could somehow see the world as it really is, through an oblong eye. If you knew the right canyons to jump in. You could – what? Fly. Or something.

The van is navy blue with Iowa plates. Five kids spill out. Not kids, he corrects himself. Five adults spill out, and he can see Milaken crouching so that a girl with a bandage on her foot can climb onto her back. Look at her. His daughter. She's stronger than Tad's ever seen her. Giant-limbed and tanned. Her blond hair a thick ponytail bouncing. Now she's cantering across the drive, piggybacking this girl who looks about half her size. She takes the porch steps two at a time. Tad opens the screen door.

She lowers herself so the girl can get down. Then she hugs him.

Behind her, two guys and another girl are coming up the steps. The girl is wearing a T-shirt with his daughter's name on it, spelled phonetically. Mĭ-lă' kĕn, across her breasts. Tad tries not to stare at it.

Bastian, Dirk, Reiley. Milaken introduces them. And Kelly.

Kelly is the girl with the bandage. Reiley is the one with Mĭ-lă' kĕn on her chest. Reiley is thin and tanned – they are all tanned, except for Kelly, who is sunburned. Reiley has skinny arms and big hands. She waves at him. She has hair like Milaken's.

Bastian looks dumb and gentle, but Tad tells himself, he's probably not. The gap between his front teeth makes him look gentle, but he's probably not. And Dirk, who looks mean and, to Tad's alarm, a little like Kent Snively, is probably not mean at all, and probably knows nothing about porches. He's not testing the floorboards when he rocks on his heels like that. He's not looking at the supports.

Tad is for a moment overwhelmed. There are too many stories tangled between these five, like a special cat's cradle – and he will never pick up the threads and play their game and understand.

Why does that girl have his daughter's name on her chest?

He opens the door to all of them.

At dinner they talk very quickly, the way they do on some TV shows, or in British movies, and Tad must accept that he will not understand everything – much will slip through the cracks. He must content himself with the odd question, if there is space for him to lean in and ask one.

So he admires the table, which he set himself, on the porch, with a white tablecloth and candles. The corn on the cob is delicious. This matters. It all matters. His daughter is healthy. She has been rock climbing in California. They have all been rock climbing – this is how they met – at Yosemite. Which, Tad knows, is that place Ansel Adams photographed ad nauseam. He leans in to mention Ansel Adams, but too late. They rush on. Dirk and Bastian were climbing El Capitan when Milaken and Reiley overtook them. Milaken and Reiley scaled the Nose in two days, Bastian and Dirk in five. *Days*, Tad thinks. He knows about the hammocks they bolt into rock, sleeping two thousand feet above the ground. He wishes he didn't.

There's a pause. They are waiting for him to say something. Two days, he says. That's exceptional, isn't it?

Milaken shrugs, but Reiley blurts: Yes it is actually.

Bastian reaches for more corn. It's amazing how much corn he's eating. He says, They passed us. Who'd have thunk it?

And what about you? Tad asks the girl with the bandaged foot. You climbed it in *one* day, I bet.

Four hours, says Kelly, and the rest laugh. It turns out Kelly is not a rock climber at all. She hiked up the back trail and met them at the top.

Tad tries to piece it all together.

Kelly is Bastian's girlfriend. They travelled all the way from Toronto, Canada, so Bastian could fulfill his life's ambition and climb El Capitan. Bastian hooked up with Dirk through a message board at the park. Then Kelly met Reiley and Milaken in the bathroom after lying in the meadow for three days, watching Bastian and Dirk inch their way up the Nose – though she couldn't see them without the binoculars, and even with the binoculars they were just these itsy-bitsy spiders, two out of dozens, all up and down that monolithic rock face.

So you don't climb, Tad says.

Kelly bends a skinny sunburned arm. With muscles like these, she says, I really should. But no.

You don't need big arms to climb, Reiley says in a tone that suggests this is an ongoing argument.

Look at these, says Milaken, lifting one of Reiley's in the air. Pathetic.

Apparently arms are unnecessary, says Bastian, two massive elbows on the table. He winks at Tad.

Big arms, says Reiley. Case in point: *five days.*

Enough with the five days, says Dirk.

Reiley leans across Milaken to address Tad. All climbing is, Mr Wilkins, is stepping. You just step up, like you're climbing stairs. What tires people out is all that hanging on with their arms. People think 'climb', and they think hands and arms pulling up a lower body. But all you really need are two legs, pushing up your upper body. You just step.

Or, says Milaken, you tip the world horizontal.

Reiley leans back. If you're Milk of Magnesia, sure, you tip the world horizontal.

Milk of Magnesia? Tad says.

Pet name, explains Bastian.

Climbing is just crawling, says Milaken, if you tip the world sideways.

Kelly only tried climbing once at the Niagara escarpment. A short climb with a top rope, and Bastian belaying her. She got halfway up and stalled. Nowhere to put her hands and feet except on the tiny ledges where they already were. Her arms got tired, started jacking at this unfamiliar frequency, out of control. Bastian was calling up to her, Reach for it, just reach for it. Reach for what? Finally she saw a clump, a jutting-out, and she lunged, her left palm smacking it and her fingers clamping down, hard. And she felt it, the most incredible thing: the rock face *rearranging itself* to keep her there.

The law of adherence, she says. You know, the way a water drop hangs onto a wood beam, or the wood beam hangs onto it? So it was with me and that rock.

After a moment Milaken says, And she never climbed again. Can you believe that, Dad?

Tad got the lowdown on Kelly's foot when they first brought her into the house. Milaken asked him for some Polysporin and a fresh bandage. When he returned from the bathroom, the foot was bare and in Milaken's lap. He saw the puncture wound on the sole of the foot, and a matching wound on the top.

She stepped on a nail today, Milaken said.

Christ.

She should have a tetanus shot, don't you think, Dad?

Hell yes.

She'd had to pee, so Reiley, who was driving, pulled over, and Kelly skittered down the shoulder and hopped a fence to go in the woods. On the other side of that fence, a rotten plank lay waiting, nails raised like hackles.

Kelly said, I felt like a compass, the kind we used in school to draw circles.

Dirk, who'd been watching from the van, said she had that look people get when they've been in a car accident. When he picked her up, the plank came with her. He could see the nail through the top of her sneaker. He had to put both his own feet on the plank, count to three, and heave her up.

What was weird, Kelly said, was that it didn't hurt. The foot that was nailed to the plank – that foot felt normal. It was the other one that felt wrong.

They help Tad clear the dishes. Milaken says they will camp tonight, under the power lines. There's room for you all here, Tad says. I know, she says. She is bent over the dishwasher. But. But what? Camp on the property, he says. Anywhere you like. Why go all the way to the power lines?

It's where she used to go, with her tent, when she ran away from home. When leaving home still meant twenty minutes away – not Chicago or Yosemite – and back for breakfast the next morning.

We'll be back for breakfast, she says.

What about Kelly? She can't walk. You're going to carry her all that way?

We'll take the wheelbarrow, Milaken says.

She thinks of everything.

Is it because he told the one-armed hiker story?

Did he really tell the one-armed hiker story, in all its gruesome detail (and, let's face it, he embellished), over dessert? He'd finally got a word in edgewise, it seems, and one word became two thousand. At the end of it, Kelly said, Maybe my foot will have to be amputated.

And Milaken had retaliated – at least it felt like retaliation, what else could it be? – with three stories about upper-storey decks in Chicago bars collapsing under the weight of their patrons. Structures not up to code. She looked pointedly at her father. There seems to have been a rash of such collapses. People falling, crushed by debris.

Reiley, still one topic back, said, I used to fantasize about being dismembered.

They all looked at her.

Worry, I guess. Worry is a better word. I used to worry about it a lot.

That's when Milaken stood up and started to clear the dishes.

Tad shuts his eyes and convinces himself his bed is in a different part of the room. This requires a certain muscle, which not everyone has, and which must be exercised regularly and built up, over time. It is not just a matter of visualizing. It is a matter of believing.

Tad trained himself as a kid by rearranging the furniture in his bedroom. Every Sunday, he pushed his bed into a new position – up against a different wall, into a new corner. He bisected the room four different ways, blocked the closet, blocked the door. Until he could move the bed around in his head, with himself in it, and believe in each new position, one hundred percent.

He taught Milaken to do the same, when she was small and couldn't sleep. With her feet pointing towards the door, he taught her to believe they were pointing at the window. Turn yourself around, he said. Keep your eyes closed. This wall – here, touch it – this is the wall with the *Black Stallion* poster.

No, said Milaken. It's the one with the calendar.

It was, said Tad. It *was*.

When she believed, when she could point with conviction to the dresser, the closet, the window, all in their new positions, he said, Okay, now open your eyes.

Feel that? he said.

He meant, did she feel herself spin? Did she feel the bed rush back to its original spot?

She nodded. It's pretending it didn't move, she whispered.

That's right.

Now Tad remembers what she said at dinner. About tipping the world. And he thinks, if his daughter can tip the world horizontal, if she can turn climbing into crawling, then maybe he has helped her, just a little. Maybe it's thanks to him.

Milaken

The wires, clasped by tall metal towers, droop and collect, droop and collect.

Where does it lead, this swath cut through the woods, grassy and straight, the towers like marks on a ruler? Chicago. Milaken can't see it, but she knows it's there.

Maybe Dirk can see it. See Chicago? she asks.

He lifts his eyes. Sure.

Dirk has eyes like the bionic man. He could see Kelly in the meadow from El Cap, when she could see nothing, not even human shapes, without her binoculars.

You lay in the meadow with a book, Dirk told her when she met them at the top. But you didn't read it.

Kelly was unconvinced. Okay. So what was the book?

Rock Climbing for Dummies.

She laughed. Nope.

It was a yellow and black book.

Maybe.

So, what was it?

Risk: A Practical Guide for Deciding What's Really Safe and What's Really Dangerous in the World Around You.

Dirk shrugged.

My dad loves that book, said Milaken.

In Chicago, Milaken slept with her toes pointing at the Sears Tower through a floor-to-ceiling window. She was eighteen, had followed the power lines to this city, where they ended, she knew, beneath this shining tower, lit up outside her window.

She lived with a boy named DJ, whom she loved. He was young, though not as young as she was, and already owned things, had money. Milaken got a job in a leather goods store. She was strong from walking all the way to Chicago. Six foot one and solid. Her body held itself perpendicular to the street, vertebrae socketed, joints flexible. She wore a jacket from the store where she worked that kept out the wind. Only her hair succumbed to the wind, and when it blew out straight behind her, she felt like a superhero.

But love meant a gradual loss of bone mass. It made you light. It made you an astronaut too long in outer space. Milaken weakened in its presence.

While DJ got stronger. Take the day he bought roller blades and put them on in the upper level of a parking garage. Holy shit, he said, when he hit the ramp. Milaken ran after him. Brake, she yelled. But he would not, or could not. He raced down three levels, picking up speed the whole way. He reached the parking attendant in his booth, half-waved, ducked under the bar, banged his head – finally flew out into the street, where a Honda Civic flipped him like a pancake. He landed on his back. Splat.

And got up. No, *sprang* up, like a gymnast, arms in the air. Ta da. I'm fine, really.

Two weeks later Milaken fell off the curb outside the Whole Enchilada and broke her ankle.

She was not a patron of the Whole Enchilada, had never paid it any attention. But that day, when she walked past, it held itself apart like a stage lit up in darkness. It was, literally, *the whole enchilada*. You stepped in. You partook. Or you fell down in the dark.

So Milaken didn't see the curb. She fell four inches and crumpled. Four inches turned her ankle black. Two of the staff from the restaurant helped her inside. Milaken sat lengthwise in a booth, her back to the window, waiting for DJ to pick her up.

You're going to get better, one of the cooks told her. He gave her an enchilada to go.

Thanks. Better from what?

Milaken told the doctor, I fell off the curb and broke my ankle.

It's possible your ankle broke, and so you fell off the curb.

Cause and effect, then, flipped.

The morning she left him, Milaken noticed for the first time that her leather jacket smelled like an animal – and she knew she would never wear it again, because it would, from now on, smell like an animal and smell like the morning she left DJ. It would smell like an animal with a broken ankle, fleeing.

She found an apartment near a climbing gym and started working out. The gym was in an old fire hall, gutted, except for the top floor, which had been converted into a restaurant called the Summit. You had to climb the walls to get there. There was a service elevator, but for staff only. All customers climbed.

Milaken climbed her ass off and ate hugely. Her ankle hardened. So did the rest of her. She was like a building going up. She was like a tower of strength.

She was chowing down at the Summit when a girl's head appeared, not far from her feet. Instead of finishing the climb, the girl stayed there, her nose on a level with the floor, fingers curled over the edge.

She peered up at Milaken. Hey there.

Hey.

A foot appeared to the girl's right, hooked neatly over the lip of the floor. And before Milaken could process that *this* foot belonged to *this* girl, the climber was vertical and standing beside her table.

Reiley, she said, reaching for Milaken's sandwich.

I'm Milaken.

The girl took a bite, swallowed. So. Milwaukee. Come here often?

It was cute then, and it still is.

For her birthday, Milaken gave Reiley a T-shirt with her name, Milaken's name, spelled phonetically across the front. Reiley loves it. Probably five days out of any given week, Reiley's wearing that T-shirt. It's so soft now, it feels like her skin.

Reiley

She stops at McDonald's on her way home from school, like she does every day, for a steamy rectangular apple pie, which nine times out of ten burns her tongue, and just when she has the pie in her hands, a masked gunman springs through the doors, dressed all in black.

Reiley has been expecting this. Her whole short life, she has been waiting for this to happen. She feels something like relief as she slowly backs away from the counter and slithers under a table.

The gunman is spraying bullets into the ceiling. Bits of plaster are dropping to the floor. Some people are screaming, but they are told to shut the *fuck* up, and they do.

Reiley holds the apple pie in its cardboard sleeve between both hands and says a prayer. Please do not let him see me. Please do not let me die.

Black boots walk past her table, pause, then back up. A hand reaches down and grabs her arm, pulls her to her feet. She bangs her head on the edge of the table. She drops her pie. The gunman is very tall. Reiley is face to face with him now. She looks up at the ski mask; she looks into the eyes. The eyes have very long lashes – and she knows from cartoons that this can mean only one thing: The gunman is a girl! The most beautiful girl in the world, judging from her eyes. The gunman spins Reiley around and points the gun at her temple. She nudges Reiley towards the door. Nobody move or I'll shoot the kid. But the voice is clearly a girl's voice. And now Reiley is just going along with it. They are working together, she and the gunman. Reiley will play hostage so the girl can get away. A car is running outside. In the parking lot, the gunman tosses her the keys. You drive, she says. Sure. Reiley knows how to drive.

As they screech away, the gunman says, Nice going in there. Welcome to the other side. And Reiley knows she will be safe. Now. Forever.

If, at this point, Reiley still hasn't fallen asleep, she makes the gunman pull off her mask, and gives her long red hair. The gunman is sixteen years old and absolutely gorgeous. Reiley is twelve. The gunman doesn't mind about the age difference.

The gunman is always saying she will never let Reiley go, but what this translates to is: I love you.

Before the gunman fantasy, Reiley had trouble sleeping. During the day, she was brave. No, not brave – because in daylight she forgot there was anything to be brave about. She walked to school by herself, went to McDonald's for pie. But at night, in bed, the old fear woke up and asked her: How could you go out there? Think about what might have happened.

Right. For instance:

Before Reiley has time to scream or run, a man with oversized arms yanks her off the sidewalk and throws her into his stinking car. Maybe he has a needle all ready to go, and he gives her a quick injection that puts her to sleep. She wakes up hours later in the basement of a farmhouse, lying on the detached back seat of a car with blood in the creases. Not her blood. Someone else's old blood.

Now that she is awake, he rapes her. No, he does more than that. Unspeakable things. Like what? She isn't sure, but they involve the breaking of bones and teeth, the tearing of skin. She prays for another injection, but there won't be one. She can scream all she likes out here. No one can hear her. She waits, knowing it isn't over until he cuts off her limbs with a saw. This is how it always ends. And she will be conscious until he cuts off her head – and even for a little while after that. It will be like what happens to chickens. Everyone knows chickens run around with their heads cut off. And so Reiley will have thirty seconds to watch her headless body, still on the bloody car seat (he has kicked her head into the corner), while he rapes her again, just a torso now, no arms and no legs. These will be sunk in concrete later, along with the rest of her, and driven, over the course of several days, to various bodies of water.

No surprise that Reiley slept little between the ages of eight and twelve.

It was her older brother, Joel, who finally taught her how to sleep. Usually he wasn't home when she went to bed. He worked overnight at the radio station. But one night, for whatever reason, he came home early. Reiley was having a particularly bad time in the 'farmhouse'. Her jaw was broken, her nails torn off – and there was a dog upstairs whining because it too was being tortured by the man with oversized arms. The thought of the dog made her cry.

Joel heard her, came into her room. Reiley?

He was wearing his Dark Side of the Moon T-shirt. It was a scary T-shirt, but not when he wore it. She loved the way all his clothes felt, thin and soft. Hers never felt like that.

He said, Scooch over. He lay down beside her. She held on to a bit of his T-shirt and hoped he wouldn't notice. What's up?

She told him everything, more or less.

Joel's fingers tapped out a rhythm on his stomach. Man, Reiley. You think about this stuff a lot?

Every night. Till Mom comes home.

You're awake when Mom comes home? That's like after midnight.

It was usually more like two o'clock, but Reiley said nothing.

Okay. Here's what I think. Say we give your bad guys a makeover. Say we turn them into something that doesn't scare you.

Like what?

Joel considered a moment. Like girls.

Girls?

Joel laughed. Why not? Works for me.

Girls. Like Michelle Furlong?

Michelle Furlong was really pretty and 'this close' to being Joel's girlfriend.

Sure. He turned his head to look at her. If the bad guys were girls, would you be scared of them?

Reiley thought about it. No.

You get kidnapped and taken to the farmhouse. By a girl. Is that scary?

Reiley giggled. No.

A guy comes into McDonald's with a gun. But it's really a girl. Scary?

Nope.

All right then. He sat up. Just change the stories, Reiley.

It had never occurred to her that she could do that.

Now here she is, ten years later, Milaken's heavy leg hooked over hers, safe as safe can be, and still, out of habit, she says the same old prayer.

Please God, let my murderer be a girl.

Kelly

They build a campfire between two electrical towers. Kelly, still in her wheelbarrow, tells them about electricity, how it generates a magnetic field, clockwise around the direction of the current. Nobody quite grasps this, so she pulls a stick from the fire to illustrate. Pretend it's a wire, she says. The current flows this way. The field spirals this way. Her movements seem magical. Smoke billows orange. The end of her stick is aflame. She lifts it like a sceptre. Electricity makes magnets.

Magnets make electricity.

But, she says. It's bad for you, to be in that field.

I've heard that, says Bastian.

Dare me to climb that tower, says Dirk.

No, says Bastian.

Yes, says Reiley.

And he is up and gone.

Reiley returns from getting firewood and says, There's something squishy in my sandal.

She sits down, slides off the sandal, and there, in the dip made by her heel, is a tiny frog.

She yelps, flings the thing away from her. It lands in the fire with a hiss.

Kelly lunges – what if it's alive? – but the wheelbarrow tips and she falls. Milaken reaches in with two fingers and pulls the smoking frog from the ashes. Dead, she says.

Dirk, watching from his perch on the tower, calls out: What's going on down there?

Dead amphibian, Milaken calls back. Then, to the rest of them: I'm surprised he can't see it.

Kelly, back in her wheelbarrow, puts out a hand. Please, she says.

Milaken drops the frog into her palm. It's dead, Kel.

Kelly's windowsill was a hospital ward for anything she found dead in the pool: frogs, flies, butterflies, and once, a bird. She arranged them in a row, with Kleenex for blankets. Last thing at night, she checked their vital signs. There weren't any.

Then she tucked herself into bed and called for her father. Kelly couldn't sleep until every member of the household came to her room and said goodnight: father, mother, grandmother. Guests, too, if they made a favourable impression, might be summoned.

Once, furious with her mother for scolding her in front of a guest (a doctor, whom Kelly admired) she omitted her mother from the goodnight list. Do not send Mum, she told her father.

Later in the night she cried because she imagined her mother rising when her father came downstairs, only to be told, No Eva, she doesn't want you.

She got up early the next morning to apologize. Her mother was alone in the pool doing her exercises. Kelly didn't like watching her mother in the pool.

I'm sorry, said Kelly.

Her mother, floating belly up, righted herself in the shallow end. The water cut her in half, just below her breasts.

Lap, lap, went the blue water. Birds watched from the clothesline.

It's okay.

But I'm going to show Dr Finch my hospital.

Please don't.

This was what she'd been scolded for.

Yes, said Kelly.

No, said her mother.

Kelly walked the circumference of the pool, checking for new 'patients'. She eyed her mother suspiciously. Kelly once caught her throwing a frog over the hedge.

The bird in your room is starting to stink, Kelly. I don't want you taking Dr Finch up there.

But I want his advice.

That bird smells because it's dead.

Bastian

The winter Bastian was ten years old, he found a spider frozen to the outer screen of his bedroom window. Each morning he woke with the sun, the frosted glass a dazzling white square, and there, at the centre, a small black frozen spider.

He leaned in and breathed on the glass. Every morning. On Saturdays and Sundays, when he didn't have to get up for school, he breathed on the glass for fifteen minutes, sometimes longer. He named the spider Buster. Get up now, Buster. Get up.

Sometimes Bastian got light-headed, and he would have to lie back on his pillow. When he shut his eyes, Buster showed up on his eyelids, a white bug in a black sky, a little sun with legs.

If he were small, small as a bug, his feet would fit into the tiny squares of the window screen and he would climb up and sideways until he reached Buster. He'd have a rope with him (dental floss?) to tie himself to the screen. With his free hands, he'd massage Buster's legs. Each one. Eight in all. He'd massage the legs until they were warm and free of ice. Then he'd breathe his breath into the spider until the spider moved.

Bastian was thinking about this very hard one morning when one of Buster's legs wiggled. All the legs were wiggling! Go, he whispered. Go, go, go! The spider came to life, rappelled down the window. It didn't seem all that extraordinary. Buster's being alive, the moment he was alive, became the natural state of Buster. Buster is alive. Buster is gone.

Bastian would forget this, the spider rising like Lazarus from his window screen. He would forget it for years, until the right person reminded him.

That will be Kelly, of course.

They will break up this summer. But three years from now, they will meet again on the subway in Toronto. And later, in Bastian's apartment, she will tell her story of the window sill, and he will remember the spider he climbed out a window to save. They will be in his bed, toes pointing at the CN Tower. And from then on, they will be married.

But all that is yet to come.

Dirk

I could do it, says Milaken.

Yes, says Bastian.

No, says Kelly, wiggling her foot. No.

They are discussing whether they could, in an emergency, cut off a limb.

Absolutely, says Reiley. But I couldn't walk away, like the hiker. I couldn't leave my arm behind in the dark.

Nobody said anything about it being dark, says Milaken.

Well, I couldn't leave it in daylight either.

Then why bother to cut it off, says Bastian. If you're going to stick around and babysit it?

You've just always wanted to cut something off, Milaken accuses her. Admit it.

Reiley looks at her. So?

Silence.

Finally Kelly says, The reason I couldn't is that I'm not sure where in this body I *am*. What if I'm not in my head? What if I'm here? And she opens her palm.

People lose limbs all the time and remain fully functional, says Milaken. They don't lose their souls.

Are you sure about that?

Don't have this conversation with an amputee. Just a word of advice.

What about Dirk, says Bastian. You think he could?

No, says Kelly. That's why he's up in that tower. He's up there because he's afraid of what he can't do.

Dirk is a tightrope walker. He will start here and walk across the world on power lines. He will grow calluses, perfect lines that bisect the soles of his feet. He will circle the globe, and when he returns to where he began, when he descends from this very tower, he will buzz magnetic. All compasses will point to him.

But for now he will sit in the tower, which is called a *transformer,* and feel his cells rearranging themselves into a new mosaic.

New Mexico. Dirk led a crew of boy scouts on a five-day trip up Mount Baldy. Six of the boys made a pyramid to untangle a bear bag cable strung high between two trees. The boy at the top had a hand curled around the wire.

Then: a sudden white crack. The sky a torn postcard.

The others weren't touched. One child only was lifted, as if by a mouth, and dropped several feet away. The rest of the pyramid, left swaying and topless, was slow to disassemble.

The boy's clothes, hair, and fingernails had melted. His skin smoked. Like Wile E. Coyote who'd dynamited himself by mistake.

Dirk performed CPR anyway. Yes, by Jesus. Burning his hands and lips. Death sticking to his teeth.

The storm cloud, a clenched black fist, pounded the horizon. Had the fist been there before the strike? Had he failed to see it?

Three days later, Dirk drove back to Pennsylvania, scalded palms throbbing against the steering wheel. His lips peeled endlessly.

The pond behind his parents' house had tested positive for something. Dirk went swimming anyway. Then he drove to his old high school, closed since '91 on account of asbestos in the walls. He sat in the parking lot, still wet from his swim, a bare foot on the brake. He put it in park. He got out.

The school looked black with the sun behind it. Dirk ran across the pavement, heedless of the broken-school-window glass: triangles, rhombuses, pentagons. He ran at the school like a cartoon character who will break through a wall and leave his own shape behind. But he wasn't going through, he was going up. No gear. Just his bare feet and hands in the grooves between the bricks. Five stories up. Don't think, just do. And only when he was at the top, a black silhouette, did he feel his shadow unattach from him and fall to the ground, trembling, elongated, rolling-pinned out.

The world is conspiring to kill us.

The air around lightning is *five times* the temperature of the sun.

That we might be touched, burned, by something hotter than the sun – who'd have thought it possible? That the sun, author of everything, would create something hotter than itself and unleash it, on us?

Tad

They are scheduled to leave after breakfast. Tad pours coffee into six mugs. He loves pouring coffee into six mugs.

He's barely seen them. Oddly, what he's realizing is not how much he loves his daughter – this he already knew – but how much he loves his house. He finds himself thinking about home improvement. Small jobs. An extra wall outlet on the stairs. To make vacuuming easier. Which he plans to do more of. And while he's at it, why not take up the linoleum in the kitchen and put down ceramic tile?

He makes three trips from counter to kitchen table, each time with two mugs in his hands. He will feel taller, he thinks, and more solid, with ceramic tile under his feet.

He sits down.

Kelly says the tunnel through her foot feels busy, like there's traffic moving through.

Tad winces.

I'm thinking maybe I shouldn't go, she says.

Silence around the table.

Then Bastian says quietly, Kelly. But.

What does that mean, Tad wonders.

Kelly nods. I know, she says. But you can't carry me, as well as the gear, through the mountains of West Virginia.

We'll figure something out, says Milaken.

The terrain's not exactly wheelbarrow-friendly.

You can stay here, Tad offers. Then, to Milaken: And you can pick her up on your way back. You're coming back this way, aren't you?

Sure, says Dirk.

Milaken is silent.

Bastian says, But it'll be two weeks.

Kelly covers her eyes with her hands, and Tad wonders what's going on – why she wants to stay, why she doesn't want to go. Is she crying, or tired, or what?

In the driveway, Bastian kisses her on the forehead. Back in a jiffy, he says.

But he will not be back. He will stay behind in West Virginia when the others leave, and he will climb his way north. He will hit the Appalachian trail and decide to follow it to its end in Georgia. It will be three years before he sees Kelly again. He doesn't know that he loves her.

And on the morning that Reiley calls Milaken 'Milquetoast', somewhere on the outskirts of Detroit, the last substitute-word she can think of for her lover's beautiful name, Milaken will not be able to laugh. She will try, and fail. They will take down the tent together, collapse it into a bundle one foot by two, just 5.5 pounds – this tent that is their *home* – and bent together over this tiny package, Milaken will tell her quietly, I'm sorry, Reiley. But.

Sorry? Reiley will say. Then, looking into Milaken's eyes: Oh. No. Please.

So that two weeks from now, Milaken and Dirk will return to the farm alone. Tad will be puzzled. And Kelly will say, I knew this would happen.

Milaken and Dirk will sleep together in the van, preferring it to the house, and no one will say a thing.

Milaken will feel herself growing strong again. Because she does not love.

But all this is two weeks from now. For the moment, Tad and Kelly are left on the porch, watching the van rumble down the drive.

Kelly says, I know. You're thinking two weeks is not exactly a jiffy.

I wasn't actually.

A jiffy is an actual scientific term. A light centimetre. The time it takes light to travel one centimetre in a vacuum. Roughly 33.4 picoseconds. A picosecond is one trillionth of a second.

Pretty small.

Yes, but.

Tad waits.

They are sitting in slightly angled Adirondack chairs, so that their legs make a triangle.

Finally Tad says, So you can divide a second into a trillion?

Kelly nods. There are picoseconds out there, is what I'm saying. So you're right. Two weeks is not a jiffy.

And Tad, when he sits down with Kelly to watch *Home Crusader*, is glad of that. May the two weeks last indefinitely, he thinks.

Bite me, Kent Snively.

Tad chuckles.

Snively is hauling up someone's kitchen linoleum and putting down ceramic tile. He *would* be. Of course, the poor bastard who put down the linoleum, several decades back, used an adhesive that has since been linked to multiple sclerosis.

Snively wears a face mask during its removal. It takes all of twenty minutes and, clack clack clack, the tile's down, and isn't the finished product lovely?

Tad has to concede it is. Dark red squares that glow with a light all their own. The music generated by the new floor brings tears to the eyes. *Home Crusader* is for many a religious experience.

Though not for Kelly. Tad has told her about his plan to put down tile in the kitchen, so they have watched this episode with particular interest. Now Kelly says, Is that really the floor you want?

The next day they drive to, not one, but four different hardware stores. Kelly's thinking is this: If you're going to go with individual tiles and not sheets of linoleum, why would you use the same tile, over and over? Tad has no answer for this.

They drive as far as Belleville because the closer towns have slim pickings. Some of the tiles are simply solid, though striking, colours: mustard seed, periwinkle, bottle green. They buy several boxes of these. But then there are the tiles with flowers. Tiles with vegetables (corn cobs!). Tiles with mountains and oceans and desert scenes. Tiles with planets and stars. Tiles of Whistler's Mother. To his delight, Tad finds a series with horses grazing. There are four different tiles in this series. He buys twelve and finds himself planning where on the floor he will put them. He calculates there will be thirty-six horses grazing in his kitchen.

He hauls the linoleum up himself and makes Kelly sit on the porch, in the fresh air, while he does it. Who knows what's in the adhesive *he* used. No doubt Snively will enlighten him in a future episode.

It takes the better part of two days to get the floor cleaned up and ready. Then for the fun part. He and Kelly are up till two in the morning playing with the tiles like a jigsaw puzzle. They put solid-coloured tiles in remote, less visible places. The horses must be visible, but not on Tad's direct route from counter to table, fridge to stove. He will not, he thinks, be able to bring himself to step on them. Corn, yes. Whistler's Mother, fine. The flowers border the edge of the room. Like a garden.

They are on their knees (protected with foam knee pads), gluing the last tiles in place, when Kelly asks, So why Milaken?

Why Milaken?

I mean the name – is it Gaelic or something?

It's a brand of cement I used to use.

Kelly sits back on her haunches. You named your daughter after cement?

Milaken Quick-Curing Cement, says Tad, a little defensively. It's the best there is. Now mind you, I didn't always use it the way I should have, back in the day. Increased the sand to cement ratio more than was wise. Sometimes. But.

But Tad has always loved cement. Especially the quick-curing kind. Gets right to business. No bullshitting around, waiting days for the stuff to harden. Cement is one of the few things in life that gets stronger, not weaker, with age. Why shouldn't he name his daughter after it?

Kelly says, But cement is a hard, inflexible thing.

Well. Don't read too much into it.

Tad places three grazing horses where he knows the microwave can see them.

What's the obsession with my daughter's name?

There's no obsession.

He is thinking, of course, of Reiley's T-shirt. He wondered at first if Reiley had some connection to the cement company. But the phonetic spelling made that unlikely. Besides, it didn't look like a mass-produced corporate T-shirt. No, it was his *daughter's* name on that girl's chest.

Do *you* have a T-shirt with Milaken's name on it? he says.

Kelly looks up at him, smiles. No.

Does anyone else have a T-shirt with my daughter's name on it?

Not to my knowledge.

Okay then.

Anything else you want to ask?

No. I think I've got it.

When the kitchen mosaic is complete, it's like walking on a map. It's like walking on a record of something. Tad considers putting down tile in the bedroom – hell, *all over the house*. Bite me, Kent Snively. He walks across his kitchen floor, and travels.

Utah

It gets dark. The one-armed hiker, who is not yet one-armed, stands facing the boulder that holds him. He can no longer feel his hand, but it is there, in the damp, fossilizing. He eats a Powerbar with his free hand. His backpack dangles off the lodged arm. He thinks how fortunate he is to be able to reach into it.

Tomorrow he will try yelling again, every half hour. Roughly every half hour. What he imagines is every half hour. His watch is on the wrist that is lodged. This is not so fortunate.

He will try again with the ropes, try to lasso the fucking boulder and move it. These are things he can do, tomorrow.

But at the end of the day tomorrow, he will eat his remaining food, all of it. He will make a tourniquet with the bungee cord in his pack and use his Swiss army knife to sever the arm. Then he will walk away from it. He will not look back as he walks down that path. Oh, to walk down that path.

Acknowledgements

Thank you to:

Burning Rockers Libby Creelman, Ramona Dearing, Jack Eastwood, Mark Ferguson, Jacqueline Howse, Mike Jones, Larry Mathews, Lisa Moore, Beth Ryan, Claire Wilkshire and Michael Winter.

My grandmother, Victoria Woods, for teaching me to love stories and always believing I would write my own.

My parents, for laughing in all the right places.

Trish (mutilation *is* funny) Bragg, for cheering me on and encouraging my poor taste.

John Metcalf, Tim Inkster, Elke Inkster, Doris Cowan and Jack Illingworth, for all their hard work at the Porcupine's Quill.

And special thanks to Stan Dragland for paving the way.

Earlier versions of some of the stories in this collection have appeared in the following journals: *Grain, Other Voices, A Room of One's Own,* the *Malahat Review, Prairie Fire, TickleAce,* and *Brindle & Glass*. 'Humanesque', 'Engineers', and 'The Loss of Thalia' were published in *Coming Attractions: 03* (Oberon, 2003), and 'My Husband's Jump' appeared in *The Journey Prize Stories,* 15th edition (McClelland and Stewart, 2003).

Jessica Grant is from St. John's, Newfoundland, but loves all provinces and territories equally. She has lived in Toronto, Buffalo, Portland, and recently moved to Calgary. Does she like where she's living now? Yes. Is she homesick? Yes. She is a proud member of the Burning Rock, a group of very hip writers in St. John's who kindly took her into their fold a few years ago. She has been a technical writer and a singer-songwriter, but this (i.e., writing stories) is by far the best job she's ever had.